Witch Is When
Life Got
Complicated

Published by Implode Publishing Ltd
© Implode Publishing Ltd 2015

The right of Adele Abbott to be identified as the Author
of the Work has been asserted by her in accordance with
the Copyright, Designs and Patents Act 1988.

Chapter 1

"Are you sure you wouldn't like some?" Grandma waved the pan under my nose.

"No, thanks. I'm good."

"Your mother used to swear by my vegetable soup."

"I'm sure it's lovely, but I'm not hungry at the moment." The lumpy, green liquid looked and smelled like no vegetables I'd ever seen. I had my suspicions that frogs or slugs might be involved.

"Your loss." She poured herself a bowlful, and joined me at the kitchen table. How was I supposed to concentrate when I was likely to throw up at any moment?

"For your first lesson, I thought we'd focus on the 'hide', 'sleep' and 'rain' spells," she said in between mouthfuls of (allegedly) vegetable soup.

My name is Jill Gooder, and I'm a Private Investigator. My father was also a P.I. I joined the family business straight from school. When my father died, I took over. But I guess that doesn't explain why I was taking magic lessons from Grandma. I'd only recently discovered that I was a witch—I didn't find out until my birth mother died. Since then, I'd been studying the book of spells which I'd inherited. I thought I'd been doing okay on my own—Grandma disagreed.

"There's really no need for you to do this," I said. "I'm sure you're really busy. I've been doing okay learning these by myself at home."

"Really?" Her gaze cut through me.

"I thought so."

"Did you now? Go on then, turn that butter to stone!" She barked.

"Stone?"

"Too slow!"

"Make this bowl float in the air!"

"Float?"

"Too slow!"

"I can — err — I can make myself invisible."

"Go on then!"

My mind went blank. I should have known this spell inside out; I'd used it enough times.

"Too slow!"

"You're making me nervous."

"Me?" She cackled. "Why would you be nervous of me?"

I shrugged.

"There'll be regular tests." She slurped another spoonful of gruel.

"Tests? I'm not very good at tests. I always freeze."

She gave me a look.

"But I suppose I could get better."

"Let's hope so."

"What happens if I don't pass one of the tests?"

"Do you really want to know?"

"Probably not."

A quick read through of the 'hide' spell told me that it was similar to the 'invisible' spell I'd already mastered.

"Make sure you familiarise yourself with the limitations of every spell." Grandma put down the spoon, lifted the bowl to her lips, and drank the last few dregs — gross! This particular spell had no time limit; it ended only when it was specifically reversed. Where the 'invisible' spell would make *me* invisible, the 'hide' spell could be used to make objects or small animals disappear. It wouldn't work on humans or sups, which was a pity because there were a few people I'd have gladly never seen again. One of them was standing right in front of me.

"I'll ignore that remark," Grandma said.

I looked at her, puzzled.

"Didn't I mention that I can read your mind?"

Great, I should have realised. I could only use the 'mind read' spell once a year, but as a level six witch, Grandma could no doubt use it as often as she pleased.

"Come on then." She thumped the table. "Have you memorised the spell?"

"I think so."

"Make that chair disappear then." She pointed at the two unoccupied chairs on the opposite side of the table. Her finger was so crooked that I couldn't tell which one she was pointing at. What would she do if I picked the wrong one? It didn't bear thinking about. I cast the spell, and hoped I'd chosen correctly. The chair on the right disappeared.

"Very good! We'll make a witch of you yet! Now make it reappear."

I did as she asked. *Easy peasy* this witch malarkey.

My cousins, Amber and Pearl, came charging into the room, but stopped dead in their tracks when they saw the look on Grandma's face.

"What do you think you're doing?" she yelled.

"Sorry, Grandma." Amber's gaze shifted to the floor.

"Sorry." Pearl also seemed fascinated by her footwear.

"We wanted a word with Jill," Amber said nervously.

"So, you thought you'd interrupt my lesson?"

"Sorry."

"Go and wait in the living room."

The two of them reversed slowly out of the kitchen.

"Youngsters!" Grandma shook her head.

"I know." I tutted.

"That includes you."

"Oh. Yeah, right. Sorry."

The second spell was called 'sleep', and did pretty much what it said on the tin. It allowed me to put a person or animal to sleep.

"Will it work on anyone?"

"You needn't think you can use it on me."

"No, I didn't mean—"

"You can use it on a child or an adult, and on creatures great and small, but the larger the target the more focus it will need."

We had to go outside to practise the final spell. 'Rain' was pretty cool, even though I couldn't imagine when I'd ever need it. It allowed me to conjure up rain clouds, but they only covered a small area. I couldn't make it rain all over the city, but it might save me having to use the hosepipe in the garden if we had any dry spells. I was just beginning to think I'd mastered it when I misjudged the positioning of the cloud, and ended up getting soaked.

Nice hair," Amber laughed when my lesson was over.

"I messed up the 'rain' spell." I ran my fingers through my hair, which was still soaking wet.

"Don't worry." Pearl patted me on the back. "We've all been there."

"Are lessons with Grandma always as bad as that?"

"She probably took it easy on you because you're new to it."

If that was taking it easy, I didn't want to know how bad it might get. "Did she teach you two?"

"Mum taught us most of the time, but Grandma used to take a lesson at least once a month." Amber cringed at the memory.

"Do you think Aunt Lucy would teach me?"

"She was going to, but Grandma said because you were a late starter, you had to be taught by the best."

"Lucky me."

"Did she say there'd be tests?" Pearl asked.

"Yeah. At the end of each month."

"Oh dear."

"What do you mean, 'Oh dear'?"

"Grandma's tests are super-hard," Amber said.

"Great." This was going from bad to badder. What do you mean there's no such word? If I can be called Gooder, then what's wrong with badder?

"You'd better not get anything wrong," Pearl said.

"What happens if I do?"

"You don't want to know."

I wished people wouldn't keep saying that. "Why did you want to see me anyway?"

"We wanted to ask —" Pearl began.

"A favour," Amber said.

I had a bad feeling about this already. "What kind of favour?"

"Can you help in the tea room this weekend?"

"I thought you'd taken on an assistant?"

"*Someone,*" Pearl said, "fired her."

"I didn't fire her," Amber protested.

"You threw a cupcake at her and told her she was a moron."

"She dropped a tray of muffins."

"It was an accident."

"On my toe!"

"It was so funny." Pearl laughed.

"Look!" Amber pointed to her big toe, which was red and looked a little swollen.

"I'm not sure I'd be much help," I said.

"You'll do great. Please say you'll help."

"I've never worked in a tea room before."

"We'll show you the ropes."

"Will there be a test?"

"No tests! We promise."

"Okay then, I'll give it a go, but don't blame me if it goes horribly wrong."

Amber and Pearl ran Cuppy C, a cake shop and tea room. The twins were part of my new family who, until recently, I hadn't known existed. Just like me they were witches, but unlike me, they'd always known they were. My new family: Grandma, Aunt Lucy and the twins lived in Candlefield, which was home to all manner of *sups*. Sup is short for supernatural, and includes witches, wizards, werewolves, vampires and goodness knows what else. I still lived and worked among humans in Washbridge, but I also made regular visits to my new family in Candlefield.

The Walrus and Hammer pub was just across the road from the offices of the Bugle, Washbridge's local newspaper. It was the watering hole of choice for its esteemed journalists. Dougal Andrews (or Dougal Bugle as I preferred to think of him) was sitting with a group of five other men—all of them loud, and most probably drunk.

After the recent so-called 'Animal' serial killer case, and in a moment of insanity, I'd agreed to allow him to do an article about the part I'd played in the arrest of two murderers. I'd given my permission on the strict understanding that the article wouldn't be a hatchet job on the local police, and that it wouldn't be published until I'd approved it.

It *was* a hatchet job and I *wasn't* given an opportunity to approve it prior to publication. Good job guys!

"Jill!" Dougal greeted me like a long lost friend. "Everyone, this is the great Jill Gooder, private eye extraordinaire."

"This isn't the article I agreed to." I waved the newspaper in his face. "You promised I'd be given a chance to review it before publication."

"I had a deadline to meet. Why don't you join us? What are you drinking?"

"I'll have one of these." I picked up the pint of beer from the table in front of him, and poured it over his head.

"What the?" He jumped up.

"If you don't print an apology," I spat the words, "I will hunt you down, and rip off your head."

"Is that a threat?" he said, as he wiped beer from his eyes. "I have witnesses."

"It's not a threat. It's a promise."

I could still hear his drinking buddies laughing when I was half way down the street.

"I think I have a migraine coming on," I lied.

"You're staying!" Kathy gave me her patented big sister look.

I was adopted as a baby. Kathy was my big sister—four years older than me. She knew about my new family, but had no idea that we were witches. I hated keeping secrets from her, but it was a strict rule that humans could never know that sups existed.

Kathy had bought tickets for the local amateur dramatics society's latest production. The Washbridge Grand Theatre was anything but *grand*. The Washbridge Dilapidated Theatre would have been closer to the mark. It had obviously been built by the first cavemen, and was now held together by dust and rusty nails. My seat felt as though it was stuffed full of metal coat hangers.

"Why do you always insist on dragging me here?" I said.

"Because you enjoy it."

"I hate it."

"You say that, but I know you don't mean it."

"Don't you remember what I said after the last one?"

Kathy shrugged, but I knew full well that she remembered.

"I said, and I quote, that I'd rather cut off my arm with a blunt knife than sit through another one of these."

"This one will be different."

"How?"

"It's a comedy."

"So was the last one—allegedly."

"You laughed at it."

"Only when the male lead tripped and fell off the stage."

It was the same crowd every time — blue rinses and dicky bows. Everyone smiled and said 'hello' to Kathy, but they all blanked me.

"What's up with them?"

"They haven't forgiven you for last time. Poor old Thomas."

"I wasn't the only one who laughed when he fell off stage."

"You were the only one who shouted 'break a leg'."

The first half of the play lasted three days short of a millennium. If Kathy hadn't told me it was a comedy, I'd never have guessed. Everyone else seemed to find it funny — I think they must have been paid to laugh. The interval came as a blessed relief.

"Before you ask," Kathy said. "No, you can't leave."

"The thought had never entered my head," I lied. "Do they have anything to drink in here?"

"Just tea and coffee."

"No vodka then?"

"No, and anyway, it isn't all that bad."

"Are you kidding? The dialogue is painful. They should have called it 'Just so'."

"What are you on about?"

"You must have noticed. Every other sentence is '*So, I went to the farm...*' or '*I'm just not happy*' or best yet '*I'm just so fed up*'. Who wrote this rubbish?"

"You're only picking fault so you can leave. Well it isn't going to work."

Kathy turned her back on me, and began to chat to the woman seated next to her. I should have been back at home, practising my spells. If I failed the test, and

Grandma turned me into a frog, it would be Kathy's fault.

"I've just remembered," Kathy said, as she turned back to face me.

"That I'm still sitting here?"

"Lizzie has started collecting beanies."

Lizzie was my niece who I loved to bits — in small doses.

"I thought she was into Lego?"

"She is, but some of her school friends have beanies, so she's decided to collect them too."

I knew exactly what was coming, and suddenly I couldn't wait for the second half of the play to begin.

"I told her that you'd show her your collection."

"She's too young for beanies."

"You wanted to buy her one for her birthday. And besides, you were the same age when you started with them."

"Are you sure?"

"Don't you remember? Mum bought you that funny looking octopus?"

"Squid."

"What?"

"It wasn't an octopus, it was a squid."

"It scared me."

"Postman Pat used to scare you."

"He still does." Kathy shuddered. "So, can I bring Lizzie over to your place to have a look at your *collection*?"

I could picture her sticky little fingers all over my beautiful beanies.

"I don't have them any more."

"I've seen them in your wardrobe."

"I gave them to a charity shop."

"When?"

"Recently. Very recently. Yesterday in fact."

Chapter 2

The second half of the play was as riveting as the first, and my will to live was slowly ebbing away. According to the programme notes, it was some kind of humorous costume drama. The only humour, as far as I could see, was the price of the programmes. Six pounds? Someone was having a laugh.

On stage, the evil duke had just got his comeuppance. The duchess had grown tired of his womanising, and had dispatched him with a dagger.

Credit where credit is due. The special effects were good. The blood that was seeping through his waistcoat, and dripping onto the stage looked very realistic from where I was sitting. And the way he fell to the floor like a lead weight—that must have hurt.

The scream was loud enough to shatter ear drums—over-acting if you ask me. Milly Brown, a friend of Kathy's, was playing the duchess. She screamed again, as she stared transfixed at the blood on her hands.

"Help!" she yelled. "Someone help!"

No one reacted at first—no one wanted to look stupid, in case it was part of the play.

"Something's not right," I said. All of my years of P.I. training had not been in vain.

As the reality of the situation dawned upon the audience, the small theatre was suddenly filled with panicked voices.

"Is there a doctor in the house?" someone shouted.

A middle-aged man in the third row got to his feet, and was soon clambering onto the stage.

Moments later, still crouched next to the prone duke, the

doctor shook his head. "Someone had better call the police."

"No need." A familiar voice came from the back row. "I've already called it in."

I hadn't noticed Jack Maxwell until that moment.

"Everyone! Can I have your attention?" Maxwell waited for silence. "Please remain in your seats. My colleagues will need to take a note of your name and address before you leave."

As Maxwell passed by our row, his gaze met mine. Had he known I was in the theatre all along? Who had he come with? I checked the seats either side of where he had been sitting. On one side was a pretty young woman about my age. On the other side was an elderly man.

It was two hours later when we were finally allowed to leave.

"Jill, you have to help Milly," Kathy said.

Milly Brown, still dressed in her duchess costume, had been led away by two police officers.

"She'll be okay. It was obviously some kind of freak accident. They'll let her go once they've taken her statement."

"Can't you at least talk to Jack?"

"Jack? You make it sound like he and I are on first name terms."

"I thought you were."

"Not unless me calling him an asshat counts."

"He has to show you some respect after what happened in the 'Animal' case."

You would have been forgiven for thinking so. After all, I had single-handedly solved three murders for him. But no — not as much as a thank you.

"He won't listen to anything I have to say."

"You've got to try, Jill, please. Milly isn't strong enough to be locked up. She'll have a nervous breakdown."

"I'll see what I can do, but I'm not promising anything."

I called in at the police station the next morning.

"There's a woman down here asking for you," the desk sergeant said into the phone. "Says her name is Jill Gooder."

The sergeant raised his eyebrows, and I could only imagine what Maxwell had said to him.

"Yes, sir. I'll tell her."

"Did he invite me up for drinks?"

"Not exactly."

"Did he say he'd be right down to see me?"

"Wrong again."

"Did he say I should go and — ?"

"More or less."

At least I'd tried.

I'd never seen Mrs V so excited. She was humming, and tapping her fingers.

"What have you done to him?" I said.

"What have I done to who?" The humming stopped, but she continued to keep the beat with her fingers.

"What have you done to Winky?"

Winky was the crazy, one-eyed cat I'd adopted from the cat re-homing centre. Yes, they had seen me coming (which was more than Winky had — sorry, bad taste).

"I haven't done anything to the stupid cat. He's in your office — stinking the place out as usual."

I wasn't sure I believed her. I couldn't think of any other reason she would be so happy. I walked through to my office.

"Winky?"

He half opened his good eye, for all of two seconds, before going back to sleep.

"Why *are* you so upbeat then?" I asked Mrs V who was still beaming ear to ear.

"I'm always happy."

She just hid it well. "Something must have happened — come on, spill the beans."

"Well, seeing as you asked, I've reached the regionals."

"That's nice. Regionals of what?"

"The knitting competition. What do you think?"

"Scarf category?"

"Scarves, seven feet in length."

"That's great. Congratulations." I guess.

"The winner gets a gold cup. If I win, I'll keep it here, so I can look at it every day."

"That'll be — err — nice."

"I've bought a ticket for you."

Alarm bells began to ring. "Ticket? For what?"

"The regional finals, of course. I knew you'd want to be there to support me."

"You don't want *me* there."

"Of course I do."

"Nah, you don't."

"I do. You'll be my lucky mascot."

"It's not really my thing."

"Your dad would have come."

She had to play the 'Dad' card didn't she?

"When is it?"

"Tomorrow. I've checked your diary, you're free."

"I am? Great. Guess I'll be there then."

My phone rang. Caller ID showed Kathy. Maybe I'd ask Mrs V if she had a spare ticket for the regionals. It was the least I could do to repay my sister for the night at the theatre.

"I thought you were going to get Milly out!" Kathy yelled.

"I warned you that Jack Maxwell wouldn't listen to me. Don't worry, they won't charge her with anything."

"They already have. With murder!"

Not even Maxwell was that stupid. "Are you sure?"

"Of course I'm sure. It's on the local TV."

Strike that. He was that stupid and then some. "Leave it with me; I'll get onto her lawyer."

"You have to help her, Jill."

It didn't take me long to find out who Milly Brown's lawyer was. A call to his office revealed that she had indeed been charged with murder, but was already out on bail. Her lawyer said it would be okay for me to meet with her the next day.

Every time I looked at my desk, I wanted to cry. The once beautiful, polished surface was now scarred by the scratches that Winky had inflicted on it in a moment of rage. He'd been angry, and although he'd never admit it, a little jealous when he'd discovered I had a dog, Barry, in Candlefield. I'd tried to get the desk repaired once already, but the man had been chased off by Winky.

I had to try again. "Hi, is that Greendale Polishers?" Theirs was the largest advert in Yellow Pages.

"Yes, madam," a sing-song voice on the other end said.

"How can we be of assistance today?"

"I need someone to repair my desk. It's scratched."

"We can certainly help with that. How did it come to be scratched?"

"A cat."

"Is the desk in your home?"

"No, in my office."

"You have a cat in your office?"

"Yes." What's so unusual about that? I bet a lot of people have cats in their office. "How quickly can you do it?"

"We could get someone to you tomorrow."

"That would be great."

I gave her the address, and agreed a time. "Just one more thing," I said.

"Yes, madam?"

"Do your operatives wear safety clothing?"

"They wear overalls."

"Are they scratch-proof?"

"They're standard overalls."

"Right. Of course. Are any of them cat lovers?"

"Sorry?"

"It doesn't matter. I'm sure it'll be okay. Thanks. Tomorrow it is then."

Mrs V was so busy admiring her potential-prize-winning scarf, that she didn't notice me standing by her desk.

"Mrs V."

"Jill! You scared me to death. You shouldn't creep up on people like that!"

"Sorry. I just wanted to let you know that someone will be coming tomorrow to repair my desk. Can you make sure Winky doesn't scare them off this time?"

"How am I meant to do that?"

"I don't know. Can you keep him out here while the man does his stuff?"

"Out here? With me?"

"Yeah."

"With my yarn?"

"It's locked away in the linen basket."

I'd bought the basket after Winky had ransacked the mail sack that had previously housed Mrs V's yarn stash.

"Can I tie him up?"

"No, you can't tie him up."

I spent the next hour finding out everything I could about the Washbridge Amateur Dramatics Society. They had their own web site, which looked like it'd been created by a ten year old, back in the nineties. I'd almost forgotten just how annoying animated gifs could be. On the front page, in huge red letters, were the words 'All performances cancelled until further notice'.

The page titled 'current production' provided a full cast list for the play I'd been forced to endure. That might come in helpful. I clicked on a link marked 'Company'. This page listed every member of the society—front and back stage. It was a much more comprehensive list, which included all of the amateur thesps as well as the back stage staff. One name in the list of actors caught my eye—Jack Maxwell.

The intercom buzzed.

"Yes?" I said.

"Jill?"

"I'm here, Mrs V."

"Jill?"

I gave up, and walked through to the outer office. Mrs V was still hitting the 'talk' button.

"This thing's broken." She gave it one last thump.

Aunt Lucy gave me a sympathetic smile. "I hope you don't mind me turning up out of the blue. If you're busy —"

"No, it's fine. Come on through."

"What happened to your lovely desk?"

"*He* happened!" I pointed to Winky who was curled up, fast asleep on the leather sofa.

"He looks so peaceful."

"Don't be fooled. He's a monster."

Winky opened his good eye long enough to give me a 'look'.

"The intercom was working fine," Aunt Lucy said, as she took a seat.

"I know. Mrs V's hearing is getting worse, but she won't do anything about it. Anyway, what brings you here today?"

"It's your mum."

"What about her?"

Since my birth mother had died, her ghost had appeared to me on several occasions. I'd found it a little scary at first, but I'd slowly got used to it.

"She's only gone and got herself a man friend."

"Can she do that? I mean — with her being dead and all."

"She can and she has. Hussy!"

Aunt Lucy suddenly spun around in her chair, and shouted at the wall, "I might have known you'd show up!"

"Sorry?" I was confused by her reaction.

"You did it on purpose! Just to spite me!" Aunt Lucy yelled.

I had no idea what she was talking about, and even less idea why she was shouting at the wall.

"Aunt Lucy?"

"Sorry, Jill. I might have known she'd make an appearance."

"Who?" Then the penny dropped. She'd been talking to my mother. Ghosts can only make themselves visible (attached) to one person at a time. My mother's ghost was usually attached to me. She must have made herself visible to her sister, Aunt Lucy, so the two of them could argue.

"I'm sorry about this, Jill." Aunt Lucy stood up. "She might as well tell you herself, now that she's here." She turned back to face the wall. "Don't worry! I'm leaving. Goodbye." And then back to me. "Bye, Jill."

"Bye."

Once she'd left, I turned to the wall and said, "Mum?"

Chapter 3

"Jill? Why are you talking to the wall?" My mother laughed.

I spun around to find she was now standing next to my desk. Being a ghost must be a real hoot.

"What's going on with you and Aunt Lucy?" I said.

"Take no notice of her. You know what sisters are like."

I did. Kathy and I were always falling out and then making up again.

"She sounded pretty upset."

My mother shrugged.

"She said something about a 'man friend'?" I pressed.

"Lucy should mind her own business."

"Do you think you should be dating?"

"At my age, do you mean?"

"No. That's not what I meant."

"I realise no child likes to think that their parents have a love life."

"It's not that either."

"What then?"

"It's just that you're—"

"Yes?"

"Well—err—dead. Can ghosts date?"

"Of course. We can't leave all of the fun to the living."

"Right. Sorry, I didn't realise. So why is Aunt Lucy—?"

The door opened. Mrs V stared at me, no doubt wondering why I was having a conversation with myself.

"Are you all right, Jill?"

"Yeah." I smiled. "Absolutely fine."

She looked around the room, and then back at me.

"Could I finish a little early tonight? I have to prepare for tomorrow."

"Yes, of course."

"Thanks. Goodnight then."

"Goodnight."

My mother had moved over to the sofa. Winky was now wide awake and spitting fur.

"Is he always so aggressive?" she asked.

"You caught him on a good day. So, why is Aunt Lucy so upset?"

"When Lucy and I were about the same age as the twins are now, we both had a crush on the same man. Alberto Belito." Her face lit up when she spoke his name.

"Italian?"

"Welsh actually. Anyway, we both fancied him something rotten. He was a terrible flirt, and used to play us off against one another. One minute, I'd be sure he liked me best, the next he'd be all over Lucy."

She seemed to zone out—probably day-dreaming about Alberto.

"Mum?"

"Sorry. I was just—never mind. Where was I?"

"The Welsh guy."

"Oh yes. He died much too young. A terrible accident involving a portable sander and a monkey."

"A monkey?"

"Don't ask. The memory is too painful."

"So? Aunt Lucy is jealous?"

"Green with it." Mum laughed.

"Are you and Alberto an item?"

"As far as Lucy is concerned, definitely yes."

"But?"

"He's still as big a flirt as ever. Of course, he denies it, but I'm sure he's seeing other women."

"Ghosts?"

"Of course. He can hardly date someone who's alive, can he?"

Of course not—that would be completely ridiculous.

"Lucy will get over it," my mother said. "She always does. Just give her a few days. Anyway, how's the magic coming along? I hear Grandma has taken you under her wing."

"She scares me."

"She scares everyone, but she's probably the most powerful witch in Candlefield. She's forgotten more than most witches will ever know. You must stick with it. Promise?"

"I promise."

The next morning, I got up an hour earlier than usual so I'd have time for a run. My fitness levels were at an all time low, and I was starting to put on the pounds. I blamed the twins' cupcakes. The park was empty except for a few dog walkers and a couple of runners.

As I ran past the children's play area, I heard footsteps behind me. Another runner, who by the sound of it was running much faster than I was.

"Good morning," Maxwell said, as he drew level.

I'd only ever seen him wearing a suit before. The blue shorts and red running vest showed off his toned body. I was struggling to catch my breath; he looked as though he'd hardly broken sweat. I was amazed he'd even acknowledged me. Still, if he could be civil, it wouldn't hurt me to try.

"Morning. I didn't realise you lived around here."

"Four miles away." He pointed in a general westerly direction. "I usually run as far as the park, and then head back home."

"Impressive. How often do you do that?"

"Depends on work. I try to manage at least four runs a week. What about you?"

"About the same," I lied.

I was struggling to keep up with him as the gradient became steeper. Thank goodness Kathy wasn't around to see this. I could almost hear her: 'Jack and Jill went up the hill'.

"So, you're a budding actor?" I said.

"Not really."

"You're listed on the Society's web site."

"I only joined a few weeks ago on a whim. I thought it might take my mind off work."

"Hmm. That didn't really work out for you, did it? What with the murder and all?"

"I can't discuss the case."

"I wouldn't expect you to." I thought it best not to mention that I'd be seeing Milly Brown later that morning.

"What about you?" he said. "Do you enjoy the theatre?"

"Not really. My sister is the theatre buff. She insists on dragging me to every performance. I'm more of a 'stay at home with a glass of wine and a box of chocolates' kind of a girl."

He checked his watch. "I'd better get a move on or I'll be late."

With that, he changed gear and sped off into the distance. Obviously, I could have kept up with him if I'd tried. What? I totally could have. Even with the excruciating stitch in my side.

"Are you the private eye?"
The man who opened the door to me at Milly Brown's house was at least six-five, and built like the proverbial. Tartan trousers are never a good look unless you're a cute bear. And nose hair — way too much nose hair.
"Private investigator." I hated the label 'private eye'. "Jill Gooder. You must be Mr Brown."
"I'm not happy about this."
"I'm not surprised. The murder charge is ridiculous."
"Not that. I'm not happy about Milly talking to you. What can you do?"
"Andy?" The woman's voice came from somewhere inside the house. "Is that Jill?"
"You'd better come in." He led the way across the hall and into a large room that looked out onto a magnificent garden. Milly Brown was seated in a white armchair.
"Jill, come in and take a seat. Thanks for coming," she said.
I sat beside her in a matching armchair. 'Nose Hair' took a seat at the table behind us.
"You don't have to stay, Andy," Milly said.
"I'm staying."
Milly sighed, and then turned to me. "Do you think you'll be able to help me?"
"I hope so. Frankly, I'm surprised they charged you."
"It's all so terrible." She wiped away a tear. "I still can't believe it happened. It feels like some kind of bad dream."
"Stop crying woman!" 'Nose Hair' said. "I told you not

to join that stupid drama group."

Sheesh and I thought I was the one who lacked empathy. Ignoring the interruption, I focussed on Milly. "Did you notice anything different about that night? What about the knife?"

"Nothing at all. It was the third performance of the run. Everything had been going smoothly until—"

I waited while she composed herself. 'Nose Hair' sighed.

"The knife was the same one as I'd used before. At least, it looked and felt exactly the same."

"Did you notice anything different about Bruce Digby?"

"No, nothing."

"What about the rest of the cast?"

"Everything seemed perfectly normal until—" She broke down in tears again.

We talked for about thirty minutes with the occasional interruption from her charming husband.

"You know the way out," he said as I stood to leave.

Back in the car, I was about to turn the ignition when someone tapped on the side window. Milly gestured for me to wind it down. She looked nervous, and kept checking the house.

"I couldn't tell you while Andy was there." She was out of breath and could barely get the words out quickly enough. "I had an affair with Bruce Digby, but it had ended. I thought you should hear it from me first."

Before I could say anything, she'd turned tail and was heading back to the house. Did the police already know about the affair? Who had ended it?

"Has the desk repair man been?" I asked Mrs V when I got back to the office.

"He has. Such a nice young man with curly, brown hair."

"And?"

"A nice smile."

"I meant has he repaired it? Winky didn't chase him off did he?"

"Good as new. You can't tell where the scratches were. His name was Andrew. I gave him a scarf."

Sure enough, the desk was back to its former glory.

"No more climbing on the desk, Winky. Do you hear me?" I looked under the desk. "Winky? Where are you?"

That's when I noticed the window.

"Mrs V!"

Deaf as a post.

"Mrs V, why is the window in my office open?"

"Andrew said the room needed ventilating because of the polish fumes."

"What about Winky?"

"What about him?"

"He's gone."

"Oh dear." She didn't even pretend to be upset.

I spent the next ten minutes checking every nook and cranny in the office. It would have been just like Winky to wind me up. Not this time. He was nowhere to be seen.

I hurried down the stairs and onto the street. I checked the road first—there was no feline road-kill as far as I could see.

"Excuse me." I stopped a man in a suit. "Have you seen a cat?"

"Lots of times."

Everyone was a wise guy.

"I meant just now. He only has one eye."

"I saw a one-legged pigeon once."

"That's great, thanks."

Fifteen minutes later, and still no one had seen Winky.

"He'll be back," Mrs V said when I returned to the office. "Unfortunately."

"How will he find his way back?" Why did I even care? I'd got rid of the psycho cat—I should have been breaking open the champagne.

I slipped the paper into the photocopier. "How many copies do you think I'll need?"

Mrs V looked at me as if I'd totally lost my mind.

"Thirty ought to do it," I answered my own question. "What do you think?" I handed the first copy to Mrs V.

"It's scary."

I'd used a recent photo of Winky that I had on my phone. The poster listed my mobile, office and home phone numbers. "Is a fifty pound reward enough?"

"I'd pay that much *not* to get him back," Mrs V said.

I ignored her comments, collected the posters, and headed back to the streets.

Chapter 4

"You can't stick that there." A middle-aged man wearing flared trousers and a tank top stabbed his finger at the poster that I'd just attached to the lamp post.

"Why not?"

"That picture will scare the kids. What is it anyway?"

"A cat. What do you think it is?"

"Why has it only got one eye?"

"It got tired of having two, and gave one away."

"You're better off without the ugly thing, if you ask me."

Before I could give him a piece of my mind, his phone rang and he walked away. No doubt the seventies wanting their clothes back.

Whatever happened to all the animal lovers? It seemed like everyone who saw the poster either commented on how ugly/scary Winky was, or complained I was littering the streets.

I covered an area of approximately one quarter mile radius of the office. I couldn't convince myself that Winky would have had the stamina to go any further afield.

Even though I was still annoyed at Mrs V, I'd still have to go to her knitting competition. It would have been more than my life was worth to miss it after she'd talked about nothing else all day. She'd told me who her main rivals were, which of the judges she thought were biased, and exactly where she intended to put the trophy if she won. I had a few ideas of my own on where she should put it. What? I'm only joking. Sheesh.

"How did it go with Milly?" Kathy asked when I rang her that evening.

"I didn't get much out of her. I think she was intimidated by her husband."

"Nasty piece of work is Andy. Does he still have the nose hair?"

"Oh, yeah." I laughed. "She did manage to get away from him just as I was leaving. Did you know she'd had an affair with Bruce Digby?"

"I'd heard rumours."

"Why didn't you tell me?"

"I wasn't sure it was true. Will it count against her?"

"I don't know, but the police are bound to find out sooner or later." I checked my watch. "Sorry, I have to get going."

"Got a date?"

"Yeah. With Mrs V and her band of happy knitters."

"You're going to a knitting club?"

"Not exactly. It's some kind of big deal competition. She's hoping to win a prize for her scarf."

"She has enough of them to choose from."

"Tell me about it. Gotta go. See ya."

I'd never been inside the Chequers Hotel before, and I wasn't expecting much. To my surprise, it was quite luxurious—for a three star hotel. The ballroom was absolutely heaving with people—the vast majority of them women.

"Jill!"

I barely recognised Mrs V. She was always smartly dressed for work, but tonight she looked positively glamorous. Everything sparkled: her dress, her shoes and even her hair.

"When does the judging take place?" I had to shout over the noise of the crowd.

Mrs V led me into a smaller side room. "I can't hear myself think out there," she said.

"I was asking when the judging takes place."

"They'll be starting in about twenty minutes. I have to take my 'baby' through to the judging hall." She held out the scarf, which had secured her place in the finals of the competition. "I need to pee first—must be the nerves—can you look after it for me?"

"Sure." I took the scarf, and she hurried across the room towards the toilets. She'd no sooner disappeared than my phone rang.

"Are you the woman who's lost a cat?" a man's voice said.

"Yes. Have you found him?"

"Is there—?" His voice broke up.

The signal was terrible, so I moved around the room trying to get a better reception. "Sorry, what did you say?"

"Is there a reward?"

"Yes. Fifty pounds. Are you sure it's him?"

"He's only got one eye."

"Great! I'm tied up this evening. Will you hold onto him until tomorrow morning?"

"Going to cost you. Another tenner."

"What? Oh, okay then. Give me your address." I had to type the address using only one hand, as I juggled phone and scarf. "OK, I'll pop around first thing tomorrow. Thanks."

Winky was safe and sound. Thank goodness!

That's when I saw it. Oh no. No, no no!

The trail of wool stretched back to the corner of the room where I'd first answered the call. The scarf must have caught on a nail or something, and had unravelled. It was now at least two feet below the regulation size for its class. I was a dead woman walking. There was no shortage of knitting needles at this event, and Mrs V would know just how to use them to inflict the maximum amount of pain. I glanced over to the toilets — there was no sign of her — yet.

I had to stay calm. If I panicked, it would be game over. My mind went blank. Come on! Concentrate! I cast the spell as quickly as I could without once taking my gaze from the toilets. After I'd finished, I said a silent prayer. Had I remembered it correctly? I hardly dared look down at the scarf.

Phew!

"Jill! Come on! We need to hurry." Mrs V was striding across the room.

I held up the scarf — the 'take it back' spell had worked a treat.

"And the winner of the scarf, seven feet in length, category is — ." The MC took the obligatory drawn-out pause.

The tension was unbearable. Mrs V was squeezing my hand so tightly my fingers had turned white.

"Mrs Annabel Versailles."

"Oh well." I smiled. "Never mind. You made it to the finals."

Mrs V threw her arms around me. "I won!"

Annabel Versailles? Oh yeah—it was so long since I'd heard anyone call Mrs V by her full name. "You won! Yay!"

The block of flats where the man who'd found Winky lived, turned out to be three miles from my office. I was amazed Winky had had enough stamina to wander so far. The smell in the stairway turned my stomach. I knocked on the door and waited. No reply. I tried again.
"What?" a voice from inside called.
"I've come about the cat."
"Wait 'til I get dressed."
Gladly.
Two minutes later, he opened the door.
"Did you bring the reward?"
"Where is the cat?"
"Inside. What about the reward? Plus a tenner for keeping him overnight?"
I pulled out six ten pound notes. "I want to see the cat."
The room was filthy—even the bacteria had moved out.
"That's not him!"
"Course it is. Look! One eye."
"It's the wrong eye. Look at the poster."
"That's because it's a photo. Things are always back to front in photos."
"That's mirrors."
"What is?"
"Mirrors reverse an image. Not photographs."
"Are you sure?"
"Positive. Anyway, I know my own cat, and that is definitely not Winky."
"He's brown."

"So is my handbag, but that's not Winky either."

"Don't you want him then?"

"No, I *don't* want him."

"Do you know anyone who might?"

"No."

All of this time, the cat had rested impassively in the man's arms.

"I suppose I'd better get shut of him then?" he said.

"Get shut?"

"Guess so."

"Take him to the cat re-homing centre you mean?"

"Nah. Waste of time. Who'd want a one-eyed cat?"

Yeah, who'd be that stupid? "What are you going to do with him?"

"Probably best to put him out of his misery."

"Who says he's miserable?"

"Does he look happy to you?"

"You can't have him put down because he looks a bit unhappy. The vet won't do it."

"No need to involve the vet."

"What do you mean?"

"Too expensive. A hammer will do the job."

"No! You can't do that."

"Why not?"

"I'll take him." What was I saying? Would I ever learn?

"What will you give me for him?"

Unbelievable. "A minute ago, you were going to kill him with a hammer."

"That was before I knew you wanted him."

"I'll give you a fiver."

"I want the full reward. Fifty pounds."

"Twenty and that's my final offer."

"Done!"

I had been—well and truly.

Mrs V was looking a little the worse for wear. When I'd left her at the hotel the previous evening, she'd been on her fifth glass of elderflower wine.

"Look what I've got!" I lifted the cat out of the basket and held him out for Mrs V to see.

"Shush!" She rubbed her head.

"Sorry," I whispered. "Look."

"Whoopee. You got the stupid cat back. I'm so *very* pleased. I've missed him like a hole in the head. Speaking of which, do you have any aspirin?"

"There's some in the filing cabinet. Bottom drawer." I held the cat even closer to her. "Look! This isn't Winky. It's a different cat. I've called him Blinky."

So sue me. I thought it was funny.

"Who's he, and why is he here?" Winky screamed at me when I walked into my office. Blinky was curled up in my arms.

"More to the point, what are *you* doing here?" I said. "I've been looking all over for you. I even put up posters."

"Yeah, I saw those. Looked kind of cute in them, didn't I?"

"Where have you been?"

"Here and there," he said. "Been sharing the love, you know."

Yuk. I didn't know, and I certainly had no desire to.

"How did you get back in?"

"I followed the old bag lady in. She looks rougher than

usual this morning. I reckon she's turning into a lush."

"Mrs V won a competition for her scarf last night. She's allowed to celebrate."

"You still haven't answered my question." Winky turned his one good eye on the new arrival. "Who is he?"

"This is Blinky."

"Really? That's the best you could come up with?"

"I like it—it suits him. Someone thought he was you."

"Me? He looks nothing like me. He's ugly!"

Pot, kettle.

"This is his home now."

"Over my dead body."

Don't tempt me. "It's your own fault. I thought you'd gone for good, and besides someone was going to kill him."

"They'd have been doing him a favour. Doing us all a favour. The world isn't ready for a cat as ugly as that."

"Blinky is here to stay, so you'd better get used to the idea."

I had planned to ask Mrs V to keep an eye on the cats, but she was fast asleep.

"You two had better behave. No fighting and no destroying my office. Got it?"

I looked from one to the other. Winky was perched on the window sill; Blinky was on the leather sofa. If the new arrival was intimidated by Winky, he was doing a good job of hiding it.

I didn't like the idea of leaving them in the office together, but I had to get going. I'd promised to go to a barbecue at Kathy's, but before that I wanted to call in at the props shop where the original knife had been purchased. Mrs V didn't stir when I left, and I wondered if she'd still be there in the morning.

"Mr Culthorpe isn't in," the spotty kid behind the counter at the props shop informed me.

"Is Mr Culthorpe the proprietor?"

"No, he just owns the place. He's gone away on holiday. He'll be back on Monday."

"Do you know much about stage props? Specifically knives?"

"I don't know nowt about owt," 'Mastermind' said. "I just sell stuff."

"Does Mr Culthorpe often leave you in charge?"

"Not usually. Jason is supposed to be here—he's the manager. But he rang in to say he'd won fifty grand on the lottery, and I should tell the gaffer that he could shove his job."

"It might be better if I call in again when Mr Culthorpe is back. Thanks. You've been—err—thanks."

Chapter 5

Barbecues were not really my thing. Wasps, flies and over-cooked meat – what's not to like? Kathy and Peter, on the other hand, couldn't get enough of them. From May to September, they averaged one every four weeks. And guess who got invited to them all? A pattern was emerging. Whenever I said I *didn't* like something and definitely did *not* want to do it, Kathy browbeat me into doing it. Did she actually hate me?

"Auntie Jill!" Lizzie screamed. "I've got a hot dog. Do you want one?"

"No thanks. I'm not hungry."

"Come and see my new beanie!"

Lizzie had cleared the middle shelf of her bookcase to make way for the beanies.

"Look, Auntie Jill. I've got five already."

"Wow! Aren't you doing well?"

It totally didn't matter that they weren't displayed in the correct order. I could live with it – probably.

"Who bought you all of these?"

"I bought this one with my pocket money, and Mummy and Daddy bought me the rest."

"I think this bear might like to go at the other end of the row," I suggested.

"Jill!" Kathy made me jump. I hadn't heard her walk into the bedroom. "What are you doing?"

"Nothing. Lizzie was just showing me her beanies."

"I like him where he is," Lizzie said, after giving the matter careful consideration.

"So do I," Kathy said. "He looks just fine there." She gave me that big sister look of hers. "Doesn't he, Auntie

Jill?"

"Fine. I guess."

"Lizzie, why don't you go and see if Daddy needs any help?"

"Okay." Lizzie dashed out of the bedroom.

"Don't you dare!" Kathy said.

"What?"

"You know what. She doesn't want to alphabetise or catalogue them."

"I just thought—"

"I know what you thought. They're just toys." She grabbed the beanies off the shelf, tossed them into the air, then gathered them up in random order and put them back on the shelf. "See! It doesn't matter what order they're in. Okay? Got it?"

"Okay, okay. I get it." That was so wrong.

"So, when does Lizzie get to see *your* collection of beanies?"

"I told you, I don't have them. Why don't you believe me?"

"Because you're a terrible liar. You always have been." She turned and walked out of the bedroom. "And a horrible aunt."

Ouch. That stung.

Once again, it seemed I was the odd one out. Everyone else appeared to be enjoying the barbecue. The smoke was making my eyes run, and I couldn't face the charcoaled food, even though I was starving. To top it off, the council had chosen that day to cut down the tree that stood on the other side of the fence.

"Why are they cutting it down?" I shouted over the noise

of the saw.

"We asked them to," Kathy said. "It's so old, and has grown so tall, it's become dangerous. Every time there's a strong wind I'm terrified it'll come crashing down onto our house."

"I'm going inside until they're done." I gestured towards the house. "That saw is giving me a migraine."

I needed a snack, so began to rummage through the cupboards. How did they ever find anything in this house? I'd have killed for a couple of custard creams, but the only ones Kathy had were in the biscuit barrel mixed in with the digestives and wafer biscuits. Yuk. I had to make do with a packet of crisps.

I watched Kathy, Peter and the kids as they played, talked and laughed together. Even though they were my family, I still sometimes felt like an outsider. I always had. Until recently I'd put it down to having been adopted, and maybe that was a part of it. But now I knew there was something much more fundamental that divided us. Kathy and her family were human; I was a sup. Discovering that I was a witch had, for the most part, helped me to see my life more clearly, but in some ways it had made things even more complicated. For example, if I was to marry a human, I'd be forced to live a lie because I'd never be able to tell my husband that I was a witch. I could marry another sup, but I hadn't yet come to terms with the idea of marrying a wizard, werewolf or vampire.

A cracking noise caught my attention. The road had been cordoned off so the tree could fall onto it without causing any damage to property. The workmen were screaming at one another—I could hear the panic in their voices. The tree had begun to lean, but not towards the road.

I had never cast two spells at the same time before, but I was going to need them both now. The 'faster' spell kicked in, and I was outside and headed towards the kids who were in the direct path of the falling tree. Kathy and Peter screamed in terror. The tree was only inches above my head and would have crushed Mikey and Lizzie before I had chance to scoop them up. Using every ounce of strength that the 'power' spell had given me, I raised a hand and deflected it so that it fell to one side of us.

Kathy and Peter were both in tears as they ran over and picked up Lizzie and Mikey. The workmen were as white as sheets as they surveyed the scene. The tree had crushed the fence, but had missed the house, and more importantly, hadn't injured anyone.

Peter was tucking the kids in bed. They seemed remarkably unfazed by the incident. Kathy, who was still shaking, was clutching a glass of wine—her second.

"I'm sorry I called you a horrible aunt."

"Don't be daft. I *am* pretty useless."

"You saved the kids. I can't even begin to thank you."

"Forget it. It's lucky I spotted what was happening."

"I don't understand. How did you do it?"

"I got to them in time. That's all that matters."

"But you pushed the tree away."

"No I didn't. I just got the kids out of the way."

"I saw you do it."

"You were in shock—you must have imagined it. Who do you think I am? Superwoman?"

"You are to me." She put the glass down and threw her arms around me. "Thank you, thank you, thank you."

Fortunately for me, everything had happened so quickly that no one was really sure what they'd seen. Everyone knew it would have been impossible for me to deflect the falling tree, so they all assumed their eyes had played a trick on them.

By the next morning, Mrs V was looking more like her old self.

"Notice anything?" she said, as soon as I walked through the door.

I looked around the room. The huge gold cup had pride of place on top of the filing cabinet.

"No," I teased, but then laughed.

"What do you think?"

"I think someone has spent all night polishing it."

I read the names engraved on the base. The competition appeared to date back to 1946.

"Only three people have ever retained the trophy," she said. "I'm going to be the fourth."

I for one wouldn't have bet against her. If anyone knew their way around scarves, Mrs V was that woman. "Are you planning on taking it home?"

"No. It's staying here where I can look at it all day long. The only time I'm at home is when I'm fast asleep in bed. You don't mind me keeping it here, do you?"

"Of course not." An image of Winky running his claws over it flashed through my mind.

The moment I walked through to my office, the two of them were on me. Winky was rubbing against my right leg; Blinky took my left.

"Back off! She's mine!" Winky spat.

"We can share," Blinky's tone was much more conciliatory.

"Why did you have to bring this loser here?" Winky gave me the one-eyed death stare.

"Why can't you be nice?" I said. "Take a leaf out of Blinky's book."

"Oh yeah — right," Winky said. "You aren't really buying this 'butter wouldn't melt' act are you? The cat is psycho-crazy. Look what he did to my leg."

Winky turned to one side so I could see the gash on the top of his leg. Had Blinky really done that? It didn't seem possible — he was so laid back — so placid.

"You'll just have to learn to get on together. Now who's hungry?"

If in doubt, play the food card. Just to be safe, I placed their bowls on opposite sides of the room.

I called Milly Brown's lawyer to check on developments. It wasn't good news. The police seemed intent on building a case against his client. They didn't appear to be interested in looking for other possible suspects. The lawyer gave me the name and phone number of Brian Hargreaves, who he thought I should talk to. When I called him, he seemed eager to meet with me, and said I could go straight over.

"So you were the understudy?" I said.

"No. I was the understudy's understudy. Kind of a second reserve." Hargreaves had a nervous twitch, which I tried my best to ignore—it wasn't easy. "Harrison Scott was the understudy to Bruce Digby. I was Harrison's understudy."

"Right. Got it." I was surprised an amateur production could run to one understudy, let alone two.

"Have you been second reserve before?"

"Yes, this is my third time."

To me, that sounded like a ploy to keep him interested, but off the stage at all costs. I was too kind to point that out. See? I can be tactful when I try.

"Milly Brown's lawyer suggested you may have information that could help her."

"Harrison Scott murdered Digby," he said.

"That's quite an accusation."

"He thought he should be cast as the male lead because it was his script."

So, it was Scott who was responsible for the fabulous 'Just So' script.

"It's hardly a motive for murder."

"I heard him say that he wanted to kill Digby."

"A lot of people say things they don't mean."

"Oh, he meant it. And, he's been in prison before."

Maybe this wasn't the wild goose chase it had appeared to be.

"What for? Any violence involved?"

"Parking tickets."

The geese were back, wilder than ever, and the chase was well and truly on.

"No one goes to prison for parking tickets."

"They do if they refuse to pay, end up with a county

court order, and then insult the judge."
"Contempt of court then? It's still a long way from that to murder."
"He's your man. Trust me on this one."

Kathy phoned to get an update on the Milly Brown case. I had to tell her that, so far, things weren't looking good. Milly was still the prime suspect. In fact, as far as the police were concerned, it appeared she was the only suspect. I told Kathy I was hoping to set up meetings with Digby's widow and with Harrison Scott, the understudy and serial non-payer of parking tickets.

"That was quite some witchcraft you pulled off yesterday." My mother had appeared in the bedroom just as I was getting changed.
"Mum!" I held the tee-shirt in front of me.
She laughed. "I've seen you naked a thousand times before."
"Maybe so, but I didn't know you were there then."
"Would you like me to wait in the next room?"
"Please."
She sighed, as she drifted straight through the closed door. Neat trick!

"As I was saying before you came over all embarrassed," my mother said. "You did well yesterday. Those kids would be dead if it wasn't for you."
A shiver ran down my spine. I didn't like to think what might have happened if I'd cried off the barbecue.
"I just acted instinctively—I didn't have time to think about it."

"To combine two spells so quickly. Very few new witches could have pulled that off."

"Thanks, I guess."

"Do you see now why it would be better for you to move to Candlefield? Hiding your powers here in Washbridge is going to be very difficult."

"If I'd been in Candlefield, the kids would be dead. I won't leave my family behind."

Chapter 6

"There's someone I'd like you to meet." My mother seemed a little nervous all of a sudden.

"Would that someone be Welsh by any chance?"

"He would indeed." She turned to one side and shouted, "Alberto!"

I wasn't sure I was ready for this. No child looks forward to meeting their mother's new love interest, and especially not when that person is a Welsh, Italian ghost. His smile was dazzling. He was a stunningly handsome man.

"You must be Jill. I've heard a lot about you."

The lilt caught me off-guard even though I'd known he was Welsh.

"Pleased to meet you," I said.

"You're as beautiful as your mother."

"Thank you." I blushed.

"There's something we have to tell you," my mother said, almost sheepishly.

"Yes?" I wasn't sure I could take any more crazy.

"Alberto has asked me to marry him, and I have said 'yes'." They looked into each other's eyes, and kissed a long lingering kiss.

Too much. Way too much. Please stop.

"You can't get married."

They both stared at me.

"Why not?" my mother said. "I know we've only just got back together, but we've known each other since we were your age."

"No, it's not that. It's just — "

"What?"

"You're — err — dead. Ghosts can't marry, can they?"

"Of course they can. It happens all the time."

Stupid me. Obviously it does.

"I would love for you to give me away."

"What about Aunt Lucy? Won't she be expecting to do that?"

"I would have asked her, but she won't even get an invitation to the wedding unless she changes her attitude." My mother's face was red with anger.

"Now Darlene." Alberto took her hand. "She's your sister. She has to be there."

My mother shrugged. "Say you'll do it, Jill, please. It means a lot to me."

"Okay, I guess so."

Give away my mother, the ghost — why not? Nothing at all weird about that. Normally, I'd ask Kathy to help me pick out an outfit — except that I couldn't because I wasn't allowed to tell my own sister that I was a witch. Or that I had a ghost for a mother. Or that I had magical powers and lived, not only in Washbridge, but also in Candlefield — a place that didn't even exist as far as humans were concerned. Or that I could talk to animals. Or that I had used my magical powers to save her children's lives.

La, la, la, la - welcome to my crazy world!

I'd had some bad ideas in my time, but agreeing to help out in the tea room was right up there with them. First off, I'd never worked in a shop of any kind — ever. And second, I was the world's clumsiest person.

I'd planned to go straight to the twins' place because I didn't want to face awkward questions from Aunt Lucy about my mother and Alberto. My car, however, had other ideas. Despite my best efforts to steer it towards the twins' shop, it pulled up right outside of Aunt Lucy's house.

"Jill! Lovely to see you." Aunt Lucy held open the car door. "Come on in."

"I'm just on my way to Cuppy C."

"Plenty of time for that. Come and have a drink with me first. We have a lot to talk about."

That's what I was worried about. Did she know about the wedding? If not, should I tell her?

"Biscuit?"

She offered me the tin, which was full of assorted biscuits.

"No thanks, I'm not hungry. How are the twins doing?"

"They aren't speaking to one another. Stupid girls!"

"What's happened?"

"It's a long story. Typical vampire/werewolf nonsense. They'll no doubt fill you in. I don't have any patience for it."

Trying to survive my stint in the tea room was going to be difficult enough without having to play referee to the twins.

"Have you met *him* yet?" Aunt Lucy said.

"Who?" Play dumb—that was my strategy.

"Alberto. Who else? I bet your mother couldn't wait to show him off."

"They came over yesterday."

"What did you think of him?"

"He seemed very—Welsh."

Aunt Lucy smiled. "He's certainly that. What did they have to say?"

What was I supposed to say now? Was the wedding meant to be a secret? My mother hadn't said it was. Still, it wasn't my place to broadcast the news. I decided to keep it to myself for now. "Nothing much."

"Jill?" Aunt Lucy could see I was holding something back.

"They're getting married," I blurted out.

Brilliant. Well done, Jill. Very subtle.

"They're what?"

"Getting married."

"Over my dead body!"

She took that well.

Amber was all alone behind the cake counter when I arrived.

"Where's Pearl?"

"Don't mention her name to me."

Great start.

"And what exactly did the person whose name I'm not allowed to mention do?"

"I don't want to talk about it."

Fantastic. And to think I'd thought my time in Candlefield would be a relaxing break. This conversation was getting me nowhere. Maybe I'd get more sense out of Pearl. I found her in the tea room.

"Hi, Jill." She gave me a mini-wave.

"What's up between you and Amber?"

"Don't mention her name to me!"

It just kept getting better.

"Do you want to tell me what's happened between you two?"

"No."

"Okay, where are the keys to the tea room?"

"Sorry?"

"The keys, Pearl. Where are they?"

"Here." She fished them out of her pocket.

"Come with me."

"I can't leave the tea room."

"Come with me. NOW!"

I locked the door, and ushered her through to the cake shop.

"Who's manning the tea room?" Amber said when she saw Pearl.

"It's closed," I said. "And it's going to remain closed until you two tell me what is going on, and we get it sorted."

"But—"

"You can't—"

"Watch me. Now, both of you sit down there."

"She's worse than Grandma," Pearl said under her breath. Her sister nodded.

At least I'd got them to agree on something, even if it was only that I was the most horrible person in Candlefield.

"We'll be losing money," Pearl said, without making eye contact.

"Then you'd better get this thing sorted out right now. Understand?"

"But—"

"Understand?"

They both nodded.

"Good. First things first. Tell me what's going on."

It took some time to get the full story because the twins continued to bicker and to dispute each other's take on events.

"Okay." I'd heard enough. "Let me see if I've got this straight. Someone has stolen the Candlefield Cup."

"The vampires," Amber said.

"It was not! The werewolves took it," Pearl insisted.

"Enough! Let's just say that person or persons unknown stole it. The vampires blame the werewolves and vice versa. Do I have that right so far?"

They both nodded.

"And this cup is for an annual competition held between werewolves and vampires? Is that correct?"

They nodded again.

"What exactly is the competition?"

Another ten minutes later, and I wished I hadn't asked. The game, BoundBall, sounded like some weird combination of rounders, football and hockey. Good luck to anyone trying to understand those rules. Apparently, the vampires and werewolves had separate leagues. The winning team from those two leagues played against each other for the Candlefield Cup.

"You two squabbling over this is just silly. I know that your boyfriends—"

"Fiancé," Amber corrected me.

"I know they're on separate sides of this dispute, but you two are witches. You should keep out of it, and apologise to one another right now."

"Apologise?" they said in unison, as though I'd asked them to cut off a leg.

"Right now."

They stared at one another, then at me, then at each other again.

"On three," I said. "One, two, three."

"Sorry."

"Sorry."

Rather half-hearted, but we'd got there in the end.

"Will you investigate who stole the cup, Jill?" Pearl asked.

"Please." Amber nodded.

"I'm not sure I should be sticking my nose into Candlefield business."

"Please, Jill!"

"Please!"

"I'll see. We should get back to work."

The twins took turns to take me through my training.

"I'm not *really* worse than Grandma, am I?" I said.

"Course you're not," Pearl said. "We were just upset. You're nothing like Grandma."

"That's good."

"You are a bit bossy though." She smiled.

"I'm never going to remember all of these combinations." I stared at the list of coffees.

"You'll be fine. One of us will be here with you all of the time. We'll see to the drinks. You'll just need to serve the cakes."

"Serve the cakes." I could do that.

"And take the money."

"Take the money." I wasn't great with maths, but I could do that.

"And clear tables."

When was I going to do that?

"And load and unload the dishwasher."

"I could sweep the floor at the same time if you like?"

"Yeah — that would be good."

Irony hadn't yet found its way to Candlefield.

It wasn't until I'd finished my training that the twins informed me that there would be another assistant working alongside me.

"I wish you'd told me that earlier. I've been panicking like mad."

"It was our revenge for you bullying us earlier," Amber said.

"I didn't bully you."

"You did, but in a good way. We needed someone to make us see sense."

"And you're okay now?"

"Yeah, we're fine now that we know you're going to get to the bottom of the Candlefield Cup mystery."

The other assistant had experience of working in a coffee shop. Next to her, I looked like the class dunce. By the time I'd finished for the day, my head was spinning.

"Barry!"

When I crouched down, the crazy dog threw himself at me, and began to lick my face.

"Enough! Barry, that's enough!"

"Where have you been?" he said. "Can we go for a walk? Please! Please! Can we? Can we?"

How could I refuse? I felt guilty at leaving him for days at a time even though I knew the twins and Aunt Lucy doted on him.

"Sure, where would you like to go?"

"The park. Can we go to the park? I love the park! Can we? Can we?"

"The park it is."

Chapter 7

"If I let you off the lead, you have to promise not to stray too far away."

The cool breeze had kept most people at home. The only other people in the park were dog-walkers and some young boys riding their bikes.

"I promise, I promise." Barry strained at the lead.

"Stay close by where I can see you."

"Okay, okay. I promise. I want to run. Please."

"Stay nearby. Got it?"

"Got it!"

I unclipped the lead.

"Barry! Wait!"

Within seconds, he'd disappeared behind a clump of bushes in the near distance. I was dead on my feet from my day in the tea room, and now I had to chase after a stupid dog. What was it with me and animals? Why did they all run rings around me?

"Barry!" I reached the bushes.

"Is he yours?" A man was watching Barry and another dog take turns to chase one another in circles.

I nodded, trying to catch my breath. "Sorry about that. He just took off."

"No problem. You're doing me a favour." The man smiled—it was a killer smile. "I get to take a break while these two wear one another out. My name's Drake, Drake Tyson." He offered his hand. He had a firm handshake.

"Jill Gooder."

"Nice to meet you, Jill Gooder."

The man was serious eye-candy. Aunt Lucy had told me

that I'd be able to sense what kind of sup someone was, and I was definitely getting a wizard vibe off Drake. Was I right? What was the etiquette? Was it okay to ask? Best not to.

"What's your dog's name?" I said.

"Chief. Yours?"

"Barry."

"Barry?" He laughed. "Sorry. Barry is a great name."

"No it's not." I laughed too. "It's a terrible name, but I didn't choose it. He was a present."

"I haven't seen you in the park before." Drake threw a ball, and the two dogs charged after it.

"I only live here in Candlefield part-time."

"Really? You are a witch though, right?"

"Yes, but I only found out a few weeks ago."

Drake looked confused.

"It's complicated."

"Maybe you can tell me about it sometime?"

"Maybe."

Drake checked his watch. "Is that the time? I have to go. Chief!"

Instantly, the dog turned back, and within seconds was at his master's side. Are you watching this, Barry?

"Good to meet you," Drake said. "Maybe I'll see you in here again?"

"Maybe." Definitely if I have anything to do with it.

I watched Drake and Chief until they'd disappeared out of the park gates.

"Barry?" Where was that crazy dog now?

I'd arranged to meet the twins at Aunt Lucy's. They must have been looking out for me because they came racing out of the front door.

"Can we be bridesmaids?" Pearl yelled.

"Can we?" Amber was even louder.

"Aunt Lucy told you about the wedding, then?"

"Yeah. *She* isn't very happy about it, but *we* think it's great. We love weddings. What about you?"

"Can't get enough of them. Have you been to a ghost's wedding before?"

"No, but it'll be fun."

I wished I shared their confidence. I had grave (pardon the pun) misgivings about the whole thing.

"Tell the twins they can be bridesmaids." My mother had appeared at my side. "That should give Lucy something to think about."

Before I could respond, she'd vanished again.

"Who was that?" Pearl said. "Your mother?"

I nodded. "She said you can be bridesmaids."

"Fantastic!"

"But there's one condition."

"Anything."

"Don't tell Aunt Lucy until I'm back in Washbridge."

The clubhouse was a small brick building on the edge of the playing fields. Aunt Lucy had made some phone calls, and arranged for the captains of the two teams to meet me there. The twins had wanted to go with me, but I'd put my foot down and insisted I go alone or not at all. The two men were waiting for me inside. I instinctively knew which of them was the vampire and which the werewolf even though there were no obvious physical clues.

"I'm Archie Maine." The vampire offered his hand.

"Jill Gooder."

"And I'm Wayne Holloway." The werewolf flashed me a smile as we shook hands.

"We both have a lot of respect for your aunt Lucy, and your late mother, so we were more than happy to meet with you," Archie said.

"I understand that you are a private investigator in the 'other' world," Wayne said.

"That's right. It was my father's business. I joined him straight from school."

"And do you think you'll be able to help us to solve our little mystery?"

"I'll do my best." I glanced over to the empty plinth. "Is that where the cup should be?"

Both men nodded, and then between them, proceeded to tell me the story. I didn't sense any of the animosity that the twins and Aunt Lucy had suggested had built up between the two factions. Perhaps they were on their best behaviour for me.

"I assume you don't have CCTV?"

"You assume correctly. The club funds won't stretch to it. There is an alarm, but it goes off every other week, so no one takes any notice of it."

"Was anything else taken?"

"Nothing at all, but then there's precious little else to steal.

"Why do you think someone would take the cup?"

"No idea," Wayne said. Archie shook his head.

"What used to be over there?" I pointed to a rectangular patch on the wall. "A painting?"

"A mirror. It was broken during the raid, so we removed it."

If I'd been in Washbridge, I'd have probably told them to buy a new trophy and to move on. Life was too short to worry about things like this. But I was keen to make my mark in Candlefield, and this was my opportunity to do just that.

"I'll see what I can find out, but I don't hold out much hope."

"We'd appreciate whatever help you could give us," Archie said. "And give our regards to your aunt."

The next day, I was back behind the counter in the tea room where I was slowly gaining in confidence.

"Yes sir, what can I get you? Oh, hello again."

"I'm sorry I had to rush off yesterday," Drake Tyson said.

"That's okay. What would you like?"

"Could I have a pot of tea for two please?"

"For two?"

"Yes please."

"Would you like anything to eat with that?"

I glanced around the room, trying to figure out who he was with.

"A chocolate muffin and a Victoria sponge, please."

"Who's that?" Pearl asked as I watched Drake make his way over to a table by the window.

"No one." The woman waiting for him was way too beautiful for her own good, with her long blonde hair and red lipstick. I hated her already.

"It didn't look like 'no one'." Amber was at my other side now. "You can't take your eyes off him."

"Rubbish. He's just some guy I met in the park yesterday."

"And — ?"

"And nothing. We just talked while the dogs played."

"Did you get his name?"

"Drake, I think. I'm not sure. Drake Tyson — maybe."

"Cool name," Pearl said.

Drake nodded to me when he and lipstick left. I pretended not to notice.

By the time we closed the shop, I was exhausted. The twins were still fresh as daisies and in the mood to party.

"Come on, Jill. It'll be fun. We want to show you the Candlefield night life."

"Sorry, girls. That's going to have to wait for another day. I need to get back to Washbridge."

"Spoilsport." Pearl teased.

Just as Amber was about to lock the door, a woman with a 'don't mess with me' expression walked in.

"We were just about to close, Inspector," Amber said.

"This won't take a minute." The woman glanced around, and when she spotted me, made straight for the counter. "You must be Jill Gooder."

"That's right."

"I'm Inspector Maxine Jewell."

"Pleased to meet you." I offered my hand, but she ignored it.

"I believe you have been asking questions about the Candlefield Cup?"

"I spoke to Archie —"

"Stay out of it. It's a police matter, and I don't want some private eye sticking their nose in. Especially not one from the other world. Do I make myself clear?"

"Crystal."

"Good." With that, she turned and walked out of the

shop.

"Nice woman," I said once she was through the door.

"Sorry about that," Amber put a hand on my shoulder. "We didn't mean to get you into trouble."

"Guess that means you won't be able to help after all," Pearl said.

"Are you kidding? Now I'm one hundred per cent committed to this case."

I was back at the office.

"Mrs V, can you try to get hold of — what the?" I stopped dead in my tracks. "What's going on?"

"What do you mean, dear?"

"That!" I pointed. "That's what I mean!"

Blinky was on her lap, his head nuzzling against her bosom.

"This little fellow? He's such a little darling."

"You hate cats!"

"I hate the one next door. This little fellow — he's just so cute."

Blinky upped the volume on his purring to the max.

"I suppose I'd better feed them." I started towards my office.

"No need to feed this little angel. I've already fed him."

Winky was sitting on my desk.

"Don't you dare scratch that desk again."

"Have you seen him?" he screamed. "He's got that old bag twisted around his little paw."

"He's being nice. Maybe you should try it?"

"Nice? Are you kidding me? He's not being nice, he's pure evil. Don't turn your back on him whatever you do."

"Mrs V seems to like him."

"She's welcome to him. Don't say I didn't warn you when he tears out her throat and drinks her blood."

"You're crazy. Now do you want this food or not?"

I gave Harrison Scott a call and he agreed to see me straight away. Maybe my luck was changing.

Winky was still sulking and refusing his food, but I knew he'd eat it the moment I walked out of the office. Blinky was still on Mrs V's lap, purring contentedly.

"I'm going to see Harrison Scott. I shouldn't be too long."

"Jill! Wait a minute!" Mrs V put Blinky gently down onto the floor. "I almost forgot. This came for you earlier." She took a small package out of her desk drawer.

It was from Aunt Lucy and the twins. The type-written card read 'Welcome to the family and thanks for helping in Cuppy C'.

I really loved my new family—even Grandma. Okay, maybe not Grandma.

I normally preferred vinyl, but the Ipod, which they'd bought for me, would be great for listening to music in the car. Harrison Scott, the understudy, lived on the other side of town, so I'd have time to listen to a few of my favourite tracks while I was en-route.

BEEP! BEEP!

I managed to steer away just in time. Another second and I'd have ploughed into the on-coming traffic. I pulled into the side of the road; my heart was racing. I must have fallen asleep at the wheel. All of this switching between worlds must have taken more of a toll on me than I'd realised.

Chapter 8

I was so shaken up by my near miss that I called Harrison Scott and asked if we could reschedule our meeting. He was very understanding, and agreed to meet with me the next day instead. I dread to think how I must have sounded on the phone—he probably thought I was drunk, or high. I drove home at a snail's pace, climbed straight into bed, and slept through until eight o'clock the next morning.

I decided to take a leisurely breakfast. My rescheduled meeting with Harrison Scott wasn't until ten. Normally I'd have called in at the office first, but instead I left a message for Mrs V on voicemail to tell her I wouldn't be in until the afternoon.

Tea and toast, with lots of jam. Just what the doctor ordered. Just one problem—no bread! There was cereal aplenty, but I had my heart set on two, or maybe even three slices of toast oozing with butter and covered in strawberry jam.

The early morning sun made for a pleasant walk to the shops. Maybe I'd have my breakfast out on the patio. While I was in the shop, I noticed that custard creams were on a BOGOF offer, so I bought four packets. Today was going to be a good day—I could feel it in my bones.

Spoke too soon.

"Morning, Jill." Mr Ivers ambushed me as I was unlocking my door. "I hoped I might bump into you."

Mr Ivers was one of my neighbours—a movie buff who had been known to bore people to death.

"I'm kind of busy right now," I said.

"This won't take a minute."

My hands were full of bread and custard creams, so I couldn't push the door closed behind me.

"I have to go to work in a minute."

"Me too," he said. "I have to be there for nine, but like I said, this won't take long."

By the time I'd unpacked my groceries, Mr Ivers was ensconced on the sofa.

"I'm starting a newsletter," he said.

"That's nice."

"I don't know why I didn't think of it before."

A good host would have offered him breakfast or at least a drink. I pretended he wasn't there, in the hope that he'd take the hint—fat chance.

"You probably know that I like to go to the cinema."

"I think you've mentioned it." A gazillion times.

"So, I have a pretty good handle on most of the new movies."

"Right."

"So, I got to thinking. What if I started a newsletter where I review all of the films that I see, so that others can read my take on them?"

"Don't they have that kind of thing on the Internet?"

Mr Ivers pulled a face as though he had a bad smell under his nose. "I don't do the Internet. You can't trust it."

"So how are you going to email out the newsletter?"

"I won't be emailing it. I'll print and hand-deliver it."

"So, you're going to hand-deliver the newsletter every month?"

"Every two weeks."

Even better. Where do I sign?

"And it'll only cost three pounds," he said.

"Per year?"

"Per issue."

"How many people have signed up for it so far?"

"I only started canvassing yesterday."

"Right. So how many?"

"Most people are very busy; it's difficult to catch them."

"Right, so how many?"

He checked his notepad. "One."

"Would that one be you?"

"Yes, but as soon as people see what they're going to get for their money, the numbers will rise. Look!"

"What's that?"

"This is the first newsletter. Let me show you." He patted the seat next to him on the sofa.

As I saw it, I had two choices: Curl up on the sofa next to the world's most boring man and listen to him drivel on about every film he'd seen in the last two weeks or —.

The spell worked a treat. Mr Ivers was fast asleep — his newsletter was on the sofa beside him. I took my cup of tea and jammy toast out onto the patio, where I enjoyed the early morning birdsong. This was the life.

By nine-thirty, I'd changed and was ready to leave.

"What?" Mr Ivers jumped when I shook his shoulder.

"It's nine-thirty." I pointed to the clock.

"Nine thirty?"

I had to stifle a laugh when I saw the panic-stricken look on his face. "You fell asleep."

"I'm late," he said, as he gathered up his notebook and newsletter.

"Bye, Mr Ivers."

"What about the newsletter? You didn't sign up."

"Can't be all that good if it sent you to sleep, can it? See ya."

Another bullet dodged.

I still had plenty of time, so I gave Aunt Lucy a call.

"Hi, Jill, is everything okay?"

"Everything's fine, thanks."

"When are you coming over again?"

"I'm not sure. I've got a big case on at the moment, but I'll get over there as soon as I can. Have there been any more developments on the Candlefield Cup?"

"Nothing. The two sides are still throwing accusations back and forth."

"Hopefully, I'll be able to help when I get back there. Anyway, the reason for my call was to say thank you to you and the twins, for the Ipod. You didn't have—"

"What Ipod?"

"The one you sent me for helping out in the tea room?"

"I didn't send it."

"Maybe the twins did?"

"I'm certain they didn't."

"It came to my office yesterday. I was listening to it when—"

My blood ran cold.

"Jill? Are you still there?"

"Yeah, I just—"

"What is it?"

"I was listening to it yesterday in the car when I fell asleep at the wheel and almost crashed."

"The Dark One," Aunt Lucy said.

I smashed the Ipod into a million pieces, and threw it in the bin.

Harrison Scott was a hipster/hippy hybrid. His glasses probably cost more than my car. No one should ever wear flip flops with fungus toe. He insisted on making me a cup of herbal tea, which I donated to the pot plant when he wasn't looking.

"How did you and Bruce Digby get along?" I asked.

"I hated him."

On the fence then? "Any particular reason?"

"He was talentless, obnoxious and overbearing."

"Anything else?"

"I'm glad he's dead."

"Did you kill him?" Don't ask, don't find out.

"You get straight to the point. I like that. No, I didn't kill him, but I admit I've often dreamed of doing it."

"Do you have any idea who might have wanted him dead?"

"It would be easier to tell you who didn't, but it looks like Milly beat us all to it."

"You think she intended to kill him?"

"Milly is a lovely person, but she'd fallen for Digby's 'charm'."

"You knew about their affair?"

"It was an open secret. She was pretty torn up when he ended it."

"Do you know for sure that he was the one who ended it?"

Harrison nodded. "Milly told me."

"Do you know why?"

"She didn't say. He'd probably moved on to the next in

line."

"Any idea who that might have been?"

"No. Pick any one from ten."

"Have you had any run-ins with the law, Mr Scott?"

"Certainly not."

"Are you sure?"

"Are you referring to the parking ticket fiasco?" He laughed. "Guilty as charged. You've been talking to Hargreaves, haven't you?"

I shrugged.

"Of course you have. Only he would be petty enough to bring that up. Is that why you're here? Did *he* tell you I murdered Digby?"

"He said you'd threatened to kill him."

"I never actually threatened to kill him. I might have said I wished he was dead because I did. And I'm not sorry he's gone."

Before setting off back to the office, I gave Fiona Digby another call. I'd tried several times before, but hadn't been able to get past her voice mail.

"Hello?"

"Mrs Digby?"

"Who is that?"

"My name is Jill Gooder. I'm a private investigator. I'm looking into the murder of your husband."

"Isn't that the police's job?"

"Of course, but I often work alongside them." Maxwell would kill me if he knew I'd said that.

"I've told the police everything I know."

"If I could just have a few minutes of your time?"

"I'm busy today."

"What about tomorrow?"

"I'm busy tomorrow."

"How about next week? Any day, to suit you?"

She sighed. "Will it take long?"

"Ten minutes. No more. I promise."

"Monday then. Midday."

"Thank—"

She'd hung up.

"Did you get my voice mail?" I asked Mrs V when I got back to the office. Blinky was curled up, fast asleep, on top of the linen basket. She must really have taken a shine to him if she trusted him to be so close to her beloved yarn.

"I haven't had time to check voice mail," she said. "Something urgent came up."

"To do with the Digby case?"

"The what?"

"The murder case I've been working on."

"No, nothing like that. The lagoon blue has been discontinued."

It sounded like some kind of code. The type of thing secret agents would say when identifying themselves.

'The monkeys are high in the trees today.'

'The lagoon blue has been discontinued.'

"Sorry?" I said. "Lagoon blue?"

She sighed and looked at me as though I was the stupidest person on planet earth. "Lagoon blue!" She held out the smallest ball of wool I'd ever seen. "I'm only three-quarters done, and they've discontinued it."

I was slowly putting the pieces of this cryptic conversation together. "You've run out of blue wool—"

"Lagoon blue."

"You've run out of lagoon blue wool, and now they've discontinued it."

"So inconsiderate of them."

"Couldn't you use a different blue? One that was close to — ?"

She gave me the kind of look she usually reserved for Winky.

"Sorry," I said. "Silly idea. How come you didn't buy enough before you started?"

"Normally I would have, but lagoon blue has been available for years. It never occurred to me that they'd sabotage me like this."

Strong words, but who was I to argue. The world of wool was a mystery to me.

"I've phoned every shop I know." She sighed. "No one has any."

"That's a shame." It was hard to sound sympathetic when in truth I didn't give a monkey's.

"*You* could find some for me." She looked at me, her eyes suddenly full of hope.

"Me? I wouldn't know where to start."

"You're a private investigator, aren't you? You find people and things."

I'd once investigated a case of sheep rustling — did that qualify me? "I'm not sure I'd be any use."

"Please, Jill. It's an emergency."

"You could always call wool search and rescue." I laughed.

She didn't.

"Sorry, bad joke. I'll see what I can do. No promises though."

Lizzie now had seven beanies. Either she got way too much pocket money or they were breeding.

"Kathy, *you* know about knitting, don't you?" I said.

"I knitted a jumper — once — if that counts." Kathy was picking up Lego again.

"Yeah, for Peter. I remember. I need your knitting expertise."

"I don't have any knitting expertise. Don't you remember how the jumper turned out? One sleeve ended up longer than the other."

"I thought that was deliberate."

"Why would I make one sleeve longer than the other?"

"Peter *is* a funny shape."

"There's nothing wrong with Pete's arms, thank you very much."

"So where do you think I could I find some rare yarn?"

"Rare yarn? Have you been overdoing the custard creams again?"

"I'm serious. Mrs V has run out of lagoon blue wool, and thinks I'll be able to source some."

"Where?"

"That's what I hoped you would know."

"Sorry. Not a clue."

"You're a great help."

"No problem. Anyway, enough of Mrs V and her wool. I have news." A huge grin appeared on her face. I recognised that grin. It was the kind of grin that said she was about to drop me right in it. Like the blind date with the nose picker.

"I've bought a ticket for you." She sounded way too pleased with herself.

"I don't want to go."

"I haven't even told you what it is yet."

"Whatever it is, I don't want to go."

"She pulled a ticket out of the back pocket of her jeans. "Ta dah!"

"A circus?"

"I knew you'd be pleased."

"I hate circuses."

"The kids want you to go."

"That's blackmail."

"Tell you what. Come to the circus, and I'll try to find that wool for you. Deal?"

"Go on then. Deal."

Chapter 9

"What's up with old misery guts?" Winky said. He was perched on the window sill, basking in the sun.

"Who? Mrs V?"

"Yeah. She didn't even curse me out this morning. She just put the food in my bowl, and poured out the milk. That's not like her."

"She's got the lagoon blues." I laughed at my own joke. Winky looked confused.

"It's a yarn situation. She's run out of wool."

"There are a billion balls of the stuff in that basket. Has she forgotten? I reckon she's losing her mind."

"Not just any old wool." Why was I having this conversation with a cat? Or with anyone come to that? "She's run out of lagoon blue wool."

"So she can use another shade of blue. What's the problem? They all look the same."

"Never mind about the wool. Where's Blinky?"

"How would I know?" Winky did a tiny, cat shrug — cute. "He spends all of his time sucking up to crazy knitting lady."

"I didn't see him when I came in."

"He's probably under her desk. Last time I saw him, he told me he had her eating out of his paw. I'm telling you, that cat is bad news."

I heard the outer door open, followed by the sound of a familiar voice. To what did I owe this pleasure I wondered. Mrs V showed Jack Maxwell into my office.

"We can't keep on meeting like this," I gestured to the chair in front of my desk. "Have a seat."

"This isn't a social call." He stared at Winky, then swivelled around in his chair and stared at the door behind him. I knew that the two of us weren't always on the best of terms, but I did expect the basic courtesy of him not turning his back to me.

"I'm over here," I said.

He swivelled back around. "He." He pointed to Winky. "He was out there."

"No, I'm fairly sure he's right there — on the window sill."

"But I saw him in the bottom drawer of the filing cabinet in your outer office."

So that was where Blinky had been hiding.

"That's Blinky."

"What is?"

"The cat in the filing cabinet."

"Who's this then?"

"This is Winky."

"You have two cats? Winky and Blinky?"

"Yep."

"Identical?"

"Not exactly."

"They both have one eye."

"They both have different one-eyes. Right and left."

"Why?"

"Why what?"

"Why do you have two one-eyed cats?"

"I collect them. Like stamps. Or coins."

He looked dazed, so while I had him on the ropes, I went in for the kill. "Do you know anything about knitting by any chance?"

"Knitting?"

"Yeah, you know, two needles and a ball of wool—clickety click." I did an impression with my hands.

"No. Why would I know anything about knitting?"

I couldn't say I was surprised; he had more the look of a crocheter.

"Look," he said. "I'm here about the Digby murder."

"What's the latest?"

"I'm the one asking the questions. I understand you paid a visit to the understudy, Harrison Scott, yesterday."

It didn't sound like a question, so I waited for more.

"So, did you?"

Apparently, it was a question.

"If you've come here to tell me to keep out of police business, you're wasting your time and mine. I'll talk to whoever I want."

"He's dead."

"Who's dead?"

"Harrison Scott."

It was my turn to be dazed. "How? When?"

"Yesterday evening. Suicide."

That simply did not compute. The man I'd spoken to hadn't been suicidal. No way.

"How?"

"He threw himself off a cliff."

"Are you sure it was suicide? Someone might have—"

"He left a note. He confessed to Digby's murder."

This made zero sense.

"I don't believe it," I said.

"Why doesn't that surprise me?"

"Have you forgotten what happened with the 'Animal' case? You had a confession then too."

"This is different."

"If you're so sure you have your man, why are you here?"

"Just routine. You were probably the last person to see Harrison Scott alive. I need you to tell me everything he said to you."

I spent the next ten minutes recounting my conversation from the previous day. Maxwell barely commented; he was just tying up loose ends. The case was already closed as far as he was concerned.

Mrs V had Blinky in her arms, and was doing the waltz—or it might have been the foxtrot. Jack Maxwell gave her only a cursory glance—I guess by now he was used to the crazy that was my office.

"Why are you so happy all of a sudden?" I said to Mrs V, after Maxwell had left.

"Kathy came through!" Mrs V smiled.

"She did? The lagoon blue?"

"Yes. She's found more than enough for me to finish off the scarf. Give her a big hug from me the next time you see her, will you?"

"Sure." Maybe Kathy should have been the one to take over the family business.

If I'd had any sense, I'd have left well alone. Milly was free, the police had their man—even if he had committed suicide. All was well with the world. But then common-sense had never been my strong suit.

It was a fifty mile drive to the coast, but it was a beautiful sunny day and the roads were quiet. A little music would have made the journey even better, but after my recent experience, I decided not to risk it. Instead, I listened to a talk radio station. They were discussing the world shortage of tuna. Better not tell Winky.

Moston Bay was a secluded beauty spot. Located between two large, popular seaside resorts, it attracted mainly the older crowd. If the price of tickets in the town's only car park was anything to go by that would have been the affluent, older crowd.

After Maxwell had left my office, I'd searched the news channels online. They'd had only sketchy details about the suicide, but they had shown aerial images of the cliffs from which Harrison Scott had supposedly thrown himself.

"The red brick road is closed," the man in the small refreshment kiosk called to me.

"Sorry?"

"It's closed about half a mile down that way because of what happened yesterday. Didn't you hear?"

"The suicide?"

"Yeah. The police have it taped off."

"What did you call the pathway?"

"The red brick road. It's what all the locals call it. The stupid council had it resurfaced with red shale or clay or something, about a month ago. Look."

There were several sets of red footprints across the car park.

"It's okay when it's dry, but every time it rains, we get this. Some of the locals reckon they're going to sue the council. I might do the same. It ain't doing my business any good."

"I'm a private investigator." I flashed him my card. He

was suitably unimpressed. "I'm working on what might be a related incident. Were you here yesterday?"

"Yeah. I actually saw the guy who topped himself."

"How did he seem?"

"Okay. We get the occasional jumper up here. I can usually pick them out. He didn't seem to fit the mould."

"How do you mean?"

"They all have the same haunted look in their eyes, and they hardly ever speak."

"Did he speak to you?"

"Just small talk. He bought an ice cream — with a flake. It was the only one I sold all day. It wasn't exactly the weather for it."

"Was anyone with him?"

"No, he was by himself. It was pretty dead all day because of the weather. A few dog walkers — that was about it."

"Do you know who controls the CCTV in the car park?"

"No one. Doesn't work. Hasn't done for almost three years."

The coastal path ran parallel to the cliff's edge. There were no fences or barriers, so anyone with a mind to end it all could have done so quite easily. It was dry, so I walked along the red path until I could see the area that had been taped off by the police. A single police officer was on duty. I doubted I'd learn much from him. Before I turned back, I walked gingerly over to the cliff's edge. It was a long way down, with rocks and shingle waiting at the bottom. You'd have to be pretty desperate to choose that particular exit route.

What could possibly have happened after I'd left

Harrison Scott to make him want to kill himself? I knew I could get up people's noses, but sheesh, even I wasn't that bad.

It was too late to go back to the office, so I made my way home. I wanted to put in a couple of hours practising spells, so I would be ready for Grandma's test. As I walked from my car, I spotted Mr Ivers talking to one of the other neighbours. Judging by her pained expression, he must have been trying to sign her up for his newsletter.

"Kathy? Lizzie? What a nice surprise."
The two of them were waiting for me in my living room. Kathy and I had exchanged spare keys in case of an emergency.
"Look Auntie Jill! We found them!" Lizzie said. She had beanies stacked high, either side of her on the sofa. "Mummy said you had lost the beanies, but we found them for you."
"Yeah," Kathy said. "Look what we found."
"They were in your wardrobe, Auntie Jill." Lizzie wiped her nose with her fingers and then picked up my favourite bear. "They were really easy to find."
"You stay in here and play with the beanies, Lizzie," Kathy said. "Auntie Jill and Mummy are going to have a little chat in the kitchen."
Before I could object or run away, Kathy frogmarched me out of the room.
"How could you lie like that?" She whisper-screamed at me.
What was I meant to say? That I was a terrible person? A

terrible aunt?

"She's getting snot all over my bear."

"That's what you're worried about? A little snot?" Kathy threw her hands in the air. "*You* are a little snot, Jill. No, strike that! You're a gigantic, green, bogey. How could you lie like that? Who am I kidding? Of course you could. You lie to me all of the time — you always have. But to your niece? How could you?"

"I don't know what to say."

"How about 'sorry, please forgive me'?"

"I'm really sorry. Please forgive me."

"No. You're not forgiven. Not by a long chalk."

"What do I have to do to make it right?"

"Let Lizzie play with your beanies whenever she wants to."

"All of them?"

"Every last one."

"I can't."

"Well, I guess we're done then. I'll tell the kids they don't have an auntie any more."

She made to leave, but I grabbed her arm. "Wait! Look, I simply couldn't bear to watch her destroy them — "

"She's not going to destroy them. She just wants to play with them."

Same thing in my book. "I know, but I can't bear to watch it. She can take them home. They're hers to keep."

"All of them?"

"All of them, but on one condition."

"What's that?"

"That you put them somewhere I'll never see them again. I couldn't bear to witness the devastation."

"Lizzie!" Kathy yelled. "Come here, please."

Lizzie came bounding into the kitchen, holding my favourite bear by its ear. "What is it, Mummy?"

"Auntie Jill has something to tell you."

Lizzie turned to me. I crouched down so we were face to face.

"How would you like to take all of my beanies home with you?"

Her face lit up. "All of them?"

Maybe I could snag a few of my favourites — I glanced at Kathy. Maybe not.

"All of them," I said.

"For keeps?"

I nodded.

"When?"

"Right now," Kathy said. "Auntie Jill is going to help us to take them to the car, aren't you Auntie Jill?"

"Looks that way."

"Thanks, Auntie Jill!" Lizzie threw her arms around me and planted a huge kiss on my nose.

"Why did you come over, anyway?" I asked, once the beanies were on the back seat of the car with Lizzie.

"I've been trying to ring you all day."

I checked my phone. It was dead. I'd forgotten to charge it the night before.

"You heard about Harrison Scott I assume?" Kathy said.

I nodded. "It was only yesterday that I spoke to him."

"I can't believe he did it."

"The police seem to believe it. He left a note confessing to the murder."

"It doesn't make any sense."

"How's Milly?"

"Relieved to be off the hook, but still very upset about

everything that's happened."

I waved goodbye to Kathy, Lizzie and my beloved beanies. It was the end of an era. The end of my childhood.

Chapter 10

I was about to call it a night when I spotted a tentacle peeping out from under the sofa. I grabbed the beanie and clutched it tight to my chest. My very first and still my favourite beanie—the squid. Lizzie must have dropped it when she was playing with them. I could call by Kathy's on the way into the office the next day to give it to Lizzie. Or—I could hold on to what was left of my precious collection. Kathy need never know.

I thought about putting it on the shelf in the walk-in wardrobe, but if Kathy saw it, she'd claim it for Lizzie. Unless—. I cast the 'hide' spell and the squid disappeared. I was about to walk out of the wardrobe when I realised I could see the squid's reflection in the mirror. The 'hide' spell worked in a different way from the 'invisible' spell. When an object was hidden by the 'hide' spell, its reflection could still be seen in a mirror. I couldn't risk Kathy seeing it.

"Sorry, little fellow." I reversed the spell, lifted him off the shelf, and put him in the overhead cupboard. I might not be able to have him on display, but at least I could bring him out whenever I felt the urge for a little squid-love.

The next morning, Jack Maxwell's picture adorned the front page of the Bugle. It would have been so much easier to hate the guy if he hadn't had movie star looks. The accompanying article was predictable enough. Milly Brown had been released, Harrison Scott had committed suicide. No one else was being sought for the murder of Bruce Digby. How very neat and tidy.

"Jill!" Christine Best, one of the few neighbours I had any time for, shouted to me as I was on my way to the car. "Has Ivers collared you?"

"About the newsletter?"

"Yeah."

"He's tried."

"I couldn't get away." She sighed.

"Don't tell me you signed up?" I laughed.

"What choice did I have? I'd still be with him now if I hadn't. How did you manage to get away with it?"

"I cast a spell on him and sent him to sleep."

"What? Oh, right." She laughed. "I never thought of doing that."

The last time I'd seen Mrs V, she'd been dancing around the office as happy as a lark. What a difference a day made.

"What's wrong?"

Her head was buried in her hands.

"Look!" She pointed to the filing cabinet.

"What?"

"It's gone!"

"The trophy? Where is it?"

"If I knew that, it wouldn't be gone, would it?"

I checked the outer door; there was no sign of damage. "How did they get in? Did you lock the door on your way out yesterday?"

"Of course I did! It was still locked when I got here this morning. It must have been a cat burglar."

"I doubt it. More likely a common thief."

"I'm telling you it was a cat burglar. They stole Blinky

too."

"What?" Who in their right mind would want a one-eyed cat? Present company excepted.

"What am I going to tell the committee? That cup has been in the competition for decades. I'll never live it down."

"Take a deep breath. It'll be okay."

"How?"

"Have you forgotten what I do?"

"Collect one-eyed cats?"

"Apart from that. I'm a P.I. If anyone can find your trophy, I can."

Mrs V buried her head in her hands again. Another resounding vote of confidence.

"Who cares?" Winky rolled onto his back, and then back onto his stomach.

"I care. Mrs V cares."

"About a stupid trophy and a psycho cat? Good riddance if you ask me."

"I *didn't* ask you. You must have heard something in the night."

"Nah. I was asleep. I had this fantastic dream about this hot little Persian. She was —"

"Enough! I don't want the sordid details."

I spent the next hour re-reading everything I had on the Digby case. It amounted to a big fat nothing. Harrison Scott had confessed, and Milly Brown was off the hook, so why couldn't I simply let it be?

"Do you think I should call that nice Detective Maxwell?" Mrs V had popped her head around my door.

"Why would you call that clown?"

"To report a serious crime."

"Do you honestly think that Maxwell will be interested in some stupid trophy and a one-eyed cat?"

Oh no! What had I just said? This was all Winky's fault.

"Stupid trophy?"

"Sorry, I didn't mean that. I'm really sorry. It isn't stupid. It's very handsome, and prestigious, and top of my to-do list."

I knew people, who knew people, who knew other people you probably wouldn't want to meet in a dark alley. I made a few phone calls, and put the word out about the trophy. If someone tried to fence it, in or around the Washbridge area, I was confident that I'd hear about it. All I could do now was wait and be patient. Unfortunately, Mrs V didn't do patient.

When Grandma had said I had to pass her tests *or else*, she'd been kidding—hadn't she? This was worse than school, and I'd hated that with a passion. I'd never been good at exams, and it wasn't because I hadn't revised. Well okay, that might have had something to do with it. I shouldn't have been expected to revise *and* keep my catalogue of beanies up to-date. I always used to freeze— exams terrified me.

I had to be at Grandma's at ten o'clock on the dot, so I didn't have much time to spare.

"Aunt Lucy?" I called through the open door. I'd noticed that it was common for people in Candlefield to leave their front doors unlocked and even ajar.

"Jill? Is that you? Come on in."

We hugged. "You've caught me in the middle of cleaning."

"I'm sorry. I'll leave you to it."

"Don't be daft. Any excuse for a break is fine by me. It's your first test today isn't it?"

"Yeah, I'm terrified."

"Don't worry. Grandma's bark is worse than her bite."

"Really?"

"No, not really." Aunt Lucy laughed. "But, you'll be fine. Your mother may be a hussy, but she was a fantastic witch. Second only to Grandma, I'd say. You've inherited her abilities."

"I wish that was true."

"Just you wait and see."

"Are the twins at Cuppy C?"

"Don't talk to me about those girls." Her face was like thunder. What had they done this time? Had Aunt Lucy found out about Amber's engagement? I waited for more but she didn't elaborate.

A cup of tea did nothing to calm my nerves.

"Barry misses you," Aunt Lucy said.

"I'll try to make it up to him while I'm here."

"It's a pity you can't take him to Washbridge."

"The lease on the flat doesn't allow pets."

Amber walked in.

"Your hair!" I said.

"Now you see why I'm angry," Aunt Lucy said.

"I like it," I said to Amber. Blonde suited her.

"I was fed up of everyone getting me and Pearl mixed up," Amber said.

"That's a good idea."

"Not as it turned out." Amber frowned.

Pearl walked in.

"Oh?" I had to stifle a laugh. "I see what you mean. Blonde suits you too, Pearl."

"See, Jill." Aunt Lucy stepped forward so she was standing in-between her daughters. "This is what I have to put up with."

"I had mine done first," Amber insisted.

"How was I meant to know you'd had it done?" Pearl said.

"Let me get this straight." I couldn't help a snigger. "You both decided to change the colour of your hair so people could tell you apart, and you both ended up with the same colour?"

The twins nodded. Aunt Lucy sighed. I laughed.

"Who's looking after Cuppy C?" I asked.

"We've only popped out for a short break. It's pretty quiet today so the new staff can cope."

The twins grabbed a custard cream each and settled down on the sofa. A cup of tea might have failed to take my mind off the test, but seeing the twins' hair had done the trick. At least it had until I realised that it was only a minute until the test.

"It's TEST time!" Pearl said.

"Grandma's tests are really tough." Amber looked at her sister and they both laughed.

"Thanks, you two. That really helps."

"You'll be okay," Pearl said. "Provided you don't get anything wrong."

They laughed even harder.

"Stop it girls!" Aunt Lucy said. "Don't be so unkind to your cousin,"

"We're only kidding," Amber said. "Grandma's tests are really simple. There's nothing to them."

"I'm pleased to hear you say that." As usual, Grandma had appeared from nowhere. "Because you two are going to be taking the test too."

The twins' faces were a picture — a mixture of horror and disbelief.

"But Grandma, we finished our studies years ago."

"Call this a refresher then."

"Grandma, please! We have to get back to the shop."

"I'll see all three of you at my house in two minutes. Don't be late."

The twins looked at me. Now it was my turn to laugh. "That's what you call Karma."

Grandma was a tough taskmaster. The test included a mix of practical and written exercises. She focussed mainly on the spells she'd worked through with me: 'hide', 'sleep' and 'rain', but also included a few questions and tests on spells I'd already taught myself. Having the twins there helped keep me calm. When I saw they were struggling too, I didn't feel quite so bad. The whole thing took just under an hour.

"Right, that's it!" Grandma announced.

"Can we go?" Pearl stood up.

"We have to get back to the shop." Amber joined her.

"Sit down!"

They did as they were told.

"I'm sure you all want to know the results of the test."

No-one spoke.

"Top marks go to—" She paused for effect. "Jill!"

"Yes!" I yelled, but then put my hand over my mouth. "Sorry."

"In second place."

The twins exchanged terrified glances. Neither of them wanted to finish in last place.

"Or should I say, in joint last place," Grandma continued. "The twins."

"Well done, Jill," Grandma said.

"Thank you."

"No room for complacency though. I expect you to maintain that standard."

"I'll do my best."

"And as for you two—"

"We really should get back—," Amber began.

Grandma gave her a look. "And as for you two. There will be consequences."

That didn't sound good.

"From now on, you'll both take every test that Jill sits."

"But Grandma," Pearl protested. "We learned this stuff years ago."

"And apparently forgot it just as quickly. You should be ashamed of yourselves for allowing a novice witch to outscore you in every department."

I was beginning to feel uncomfortable. Although I was delighted with my test results, I hadn't wanted to drop the twins in it.

"Sorry, Grandma," Pearl said.

"Sorry," Amber echoed.

Outside, it was my turn to apologise. "I'm really sorry girls. I didn't mean for any of that to happen."

"It's okay." Amber gave me a hug. "It isn't your fault."
Pearl joined in the group hug. "It's our own fault, Jill. You did really well."
"Does that mean I'm a fully fledged witch now?" I grinned.
"Not by a long chalk, young lady!" Grandma appeared and then disappeared just as quickly.
"We'd better get back," Pearl said.
"I can give you a hand if you like?" I offered.
"Don't you have to get back to Washbridge?"
"No. I'm going to stay for a while. Besides, it's the least I can do after this morning."

Chapter 11

I'd noticed Amber still wasn't wearing her engagement ring.

"Haven't you had your ring resized yet?" I asked during a lull in the tea room.

"Oh yeah. It fits perfectly now."

I glanced at her bare finger.

"I'm still working up the nerve to tell Mum. I was all set to tell her, but then your mum got engaged to Alberto."

I laughed. "I see what you mean. Probably not the best time."

"You're not kidding. Mum went ballistic when she found out. I'm going to let things blow over before I say anything."

The chime on the door announced a new customer.

"Yes, sir," I greeted the handsome young werewolf. I was getting much better at identifying the different types of sup.

"Hello gorgeous." He flashed a mouthful of teeth.

Gorgeous huh? I'd still got it after all.

"Hi there handsome," Amber called from over my shoulder.

I should have realised he wasn't talking to me.

"Jill, this is William. My fiancé."

Of course. Now I recognised him. Amber had shown me his photo.

"William, this is my cousin, Jill."

He offered his hand. "I've heard a lot about you. Being a private investigator must be really cool."

"Not as cool as serving afternoon tea."

He laughed.

"Can I get you anything?" I offered.

"It's okay. I'll see to it," Amber said. "Grab a window seat, William, and I'll join you."

"He's even better looking in real life," I whispered once he was at the table.

"He is, isn't he?" Amber beamed. "Why don't you join us? You're due a break."

The shop was quiet so I took her up on the offer while Jean, one of the part-time assistants watched the counter.

"Grandma is making us do tests again," Amber complained.

William laughed.

"It isn't funny."

"It is kinda."

"I'm afraid that's my fault." I took a bite of strawberry muffin. Hmm delicious.

"It's not your fault," Amber said. "It's Grandma. She's just plain cruel."

The door chime rang. Pearl walked in arm in arm with her young man, Alan, who was a vampire.

"If it isn't banana man," Alan said when he spotted William.

"Mind if we join you?" Pearl said.

"Yes," Amber huffed.

"Tough!"

Alan placed his order at the counter and then he and Pearl squeezed in at our table. Judging by the way the two young men were glaring at one another, there was no love lost between them.

"Maybe I should get back to work?" I said.

"No!"

"No!"

The twins were, for once, in agreement.

I hated silence, and for several long moments, you could have cut the atmosphere with a knife.

"Well." I was the first to crack. "This is nice." Had I *really* just said that?

"It was until *they* arrived," Amber said.

"Are you and Alan planning on getting engaged too?" I asked Pearl.

"As soon as we find the right ring." She looked at her sister. "*We* don't want to rush into it and end up with something cheap and nasty."

The claws were well and truly out now.

"I'm sure there are plenty to choose from in the pawn shop," Amber shot back.

Meow!

Silence descended again, and this time I knew better than to break it.

"Do you think Alan and I could come over to Washbridge some time?" Pearl asked.

"I guess —" I began.

"William and me would like to come over too, if that's okay," Amber chipped in.

Over my dead body were those four coming to Washbridge together. But how could I say yes to one couple and not the other?

"My cat's sick." What? It was the best I could come up.

"What's wrong with him?"

"He has a poorly eye. It's contagious. Very contagious."

"Poor thing," Amber said.

"Could we come over when he's better?" Pearl asked.

"Sure. We'll sort something out then."

Another excruciating silence followed.

"Any news on the trophy?" I'd cracked again.

"Ask him!" William pointed an accusing finger at Alan.

"How would I know?" Alan retaliated. "Your people have it."

"That's a lie." William was on his feet.

"You're the liar!" Alan stood up.

"Stop it!" Amber tugged at William's arm.

"Alan!" Pearl snapped.

The two men sat down, but continued to glare at one another.

I gleaned from their reactions that the trophy was still AWOL and that both sides, vampires and werewolves, continued to blame one another.

After the longest tea break of my life, the two young men eventually went their separate ways.

"I guess a joint wedding is out of the question?" I said.

The twins laughed.

"I'd better get back to work," Pearl said. "Will I see you later, Jill?"

"Yeah. I'll be staying in Candlefield for a while."

"I'm sorry about all that," Amber said, after her sister was out of earshot. "That must have been horrible for you."

"Has there always been so much animosity between your boyfriends?"

"William and Alan used to get along together really well before all of this blew up. They knew one another long before they started dating us. Everything changed after the trophy went missing."

"Who do you think is responsible?"

"I have to side with William out of loyalty, but the truth

is either side could have done it. They're as bad as one another." She hesitated for a moment. "Don't tell William I said that will you?"

"Your secret is safe with me."

There was a steady stream of customers into the tea room. During a lull, I cleared and wiped down the tables.

"Come and join me," an old man called to me. He was seated alone at a corner table.

"I'm sorry, I have to work."

"Your partner can manage for a few minutes." He gestured towards Jean who nodded to indicate she'd be okay.

"I'm Pop," he said, through a toothy grin.

"Nice to meet you, Pop. I'm Jill."

I offered my hand, expecting a handshake, but he put it to his lips and kissed it.

"I understand that you're the newest witch in Candlefield."

"Quite possibly."

"I knew your mother."

"Really?"

"A lovely lady. She'll be missed."

"I'm afraid I didn't know her all that well."

"So I understand. You have rather an unusual story."

"You're right there."

"And you're still living among the humans?"

"I split my time between there and Candlefield."

"What's a private investigator doing working in a tea room?"

"I've been asking myself the same question."

"I hear you have a case here in Candlefield."

"The Candlefield Cup? Yeah, but I haven't made much headway. The local police have warned me off."

He smiled. "If you're anything like your mother, I doubt that will stop you."

"Someone needs to find that cup. And soon. There seems to be an awful lot of bad feeling around."

"The vampires and werewolves aren't the ones who should be complaining."

"What do you mean?"

"The men you were sitting with earlier are probably too young to remember, but the Candlefield Cup used to be a three-way competition: vampires, werewolves and wizards."

I knew the old guy was a wizard, but the revelation about the cup came as a surprise. "Why isn't it now?"

"That's a very good question. Just over a decade ago, there was a widespread disease in Candlefield that only affected the wizard population. The wizard team was forced to withdraw from the competition for two years, but then, when the crisis had passed, the other two teams used their vetos to block the wizards' re-entry into the competition."

Even in Candlefield, there was no escape from politics and discrimination it seemed. "That must have gone down well!"

"Like a lead balloon."

"It does seem unfair."

I talked to Pop for the next twenty minutes before he went on his way. As things were still quiet, Amber said I could leave.

Barry was his usual subdued self.

"Jill! Where have you been? Jill! Can we go for a walk? Can we go to the park? Can we? Can we go now? Can we?"

"Okay, okay. Let me stand up then."

As soon as I'd walked through the door, he'd hit me with such force that I'd ended up flat on my back. Then he'd jumped on top of me and begun to frantically lick my face.

"Let's go, let's go!"

He dragged me to the park—his favourite haunt. Once there, and against my better judgement, I let him off his lead.

"I hoped I might bump into you again." The voice startled me. I turned around to see Drake Tyson dressed in jeans and a white polo shirt. I approved.

"Where's your dog?" I asked.

"He had his walk earlier. I just fancied a little fresh air. I haven't seen you for a few days."

"Not since the tea room." Not that I was keeping track or anything.

"Oh yes. It was your first day, wasn't it? How did you get on?"

"I struggled. Amber and Pearl, my cousins, did most of the work."

"I didn't stop to talk to you because I could see you were busy. To be honest, tea rooms aren't really my thing, but my sister wanted to go."

"Your sister? Oh, yeah. I think I might have seen her with you." I was going for nonchalant.

"Looks like you've lost your dog." He glanced around.

I'd been so pleased to discover that the woman with

Drake at the tea room was his sister that I'd quite forgotten about my four-legged, best friend.

"I'd better go and look for him."

"I'll help, if you like?"

Yeah, baby. "If you don't have anything else you have to do?" Still playing it cool.

We walked down the hill, and headed towards the boating lake.

"Oh dear." Drake laughed.

"What?"

"Over there. In the lake."

Oh dear was right. Barry was doggy paddling his way across.

"Barry!" I yelled as I approached.

"You really do need to come up with a better name for him." Drake grinned.

"Wait! Barry!" I yelled. "Don't do that!"

Too late! He'd jumped out of the water, and shaken himself from head to tail, soaking Drake and me.

"Thanks, Barry." I said, brushing the water off my jeans.

Drake's white polo shirt was clinging to his chest. Not that I was looking — at all — not even once.

"Do you want to come back to my place to dry off?" he asked.

I was tempted, *so* very tempted, but I couldn't imagine what kind of carnage would ensue with Barry and Drake's dog running riot in the house.

"Thanks, but I should be getting back. I'm really sorry about your jeans and tee shirt." Not all that sorry, if I'm honest. "You'll have to let me buy you a drink and a cake next time you come into the tea room."

"I have a better idea," he said. "It's been a while since I

visited the human world. How about I meet up with you there? We could get a coffee or maybe even dinner?"

Was that a date? It sounded like a date, but then it was so long since I'd been asked out on a date that I wasn't sure.

"Sounds good. I'll give you my office address."

"No need. I'll find you."

I watched Drake and his wet polo shirt until he was out of sight.

"Do you like him?" Barry asked.

Although I was slowly getting used to the idea of talking to animals, I drew the line at discussing my love life—or potential love life.

"Drake seems like a nice man. Now, we'd better get you home and get the hair-dryer on you."

"Jill was with a man!" Barry blurted out, as soon as we walked through the door.

"*Was* she?" Amber giggled.

"Tell us more!" Pearl demanded.

At least the twins seemed to be back on speaking terms.

"There's nothing to tell. Just someone I bumped into in the park." I shrugged.

"It was the same man as last time," Barry said.

"*Really?*" the twins said, in unison.

"Come on Barry." I grabbed him by the collar before he could say any more. "You have an urgent appointment with a hair-dryer."

Chapter 12

I'd learned a lot from my dad. One of his favourite sayings had been *'don't overlook the obvious'*. With that in mind, the next morning, I decided to pay a visit to all of the trophy shops in Candlefield. Fortunately for me there were only three listed. I felt bad not taking Barry along for the walk, but I didn't know how long I'd be inside the shops, and I was worried he might get restless waiting outside and do something silly.

I was useless at finding my way around. It didn't help that none of the normal (human) laws of distance or even direction seemed to apply. After two false starts when I'd ended up back where I'd started, I went back to Aunt Lucy's house.

"Jill? That was quick. I didn't expect you back yet."

"I haven't even started." I sighed. "How do you find your way around this place? I keep getting lost. I can see the shops on the street map, but when I try to follow the directions, I end up somewhere completely different."

"No one bothers with maps in Candlefield."

"They don't?"

"Waste of time."

"So what do you do?"

"It's really simple. Just think of your destination and start walking. You'll be there in no time at all."

That all sounded a bit hippy dippy, but then I had found Aunt Lucy's house by allowing the car to take me where it wanted. What did I have to lose?

It felt unnatural—having no plan and no map to consult. Every time I reached a corner, I let my feet take me wherever they wanted. Ten minutes later, I was standing outside 'Merry Trophies'.

The shop was named after Mr Merry. Except that he wasn't—merry that is. In fact he was easily the most miserable person I'd encountered in Candlefield so far. Somehow, I could sense he was an angel—don't ask me how. He was the first angel I'd met, and had an unusual dress-sense. Odd socks, baggy yellow trousers and a pink hoody were not a look I'd typically associate with an angel, but what did I know?

"I don't buy second-hand," he informed me while picking his teeth. "All my stock comes direct from the manufacturers. Take a look around if you like."

I did, and it didn't take me long to rule him out of my enquiries.

Total Trophies was a much larger establishment. An eager young wizard with a huge smile and a 'How May I Help You?' badge was only too eager to show me around. He repeated the story that Pop had told me— about how the wizards had been excluded from the Candlefield Cup. I was suitably sympathetic. There was no sign of the missing trophy.

It had been a long morning. Thanks to the young wizard, I now knew way more about the trophy business than was healthy.

I was tempted by the sandwiches in the window of 'Ashes Sandwich Emporium', which was a grand name for a shop no bigger than my walk-in wardrobe. But it was the smell of pizza which finally won out. 'Magic Pizza' was running a special offer of a free drink with every medium pizza. It was too good to resist.

"Can I help?" A young witch with green lipstick and

purple fingernails asked.

"Where's the menu, please?"

"There isn't one." She smiled, and something told me she'd been asked that same question a thousand times before. "That's the 'magic' in Magic Pizza."

"It is?" I was still none the wiser.

"The oven knows exactly what pizza will be ideal for you today."

"That's very clever. What if it gets it wrong?"

"It never does."

Although still sceptical, I was prepared to give it a whirl. "Go for it!"

The whole process was very secretive, and if I'm honest, a little exciting. I didn't get to see the pizza until I opened the box.

Ham and pineapple!

"Well?" the young witch asked.

"Spot on! Thanks."

Feeling completely stuffed on pizza, I made my way to the final shop on my list—'DDDD Trophies'. That was an awful lot of 'D's.

The shop was dirty, untidy and generally unwelcoming. So was the man behind the counter, a vampire with scary eyes and a face that not even his mother could have loved.

"Hi," I said.

He grunted something, which might or might not have been a greeting.

"What's the story behind the shop's name?" A little small talk could sometimes oil the wheels.

"It's my name."

"Huh?"

"Ford."

"Ford?" This wasn't going as well as I'd hoped.

"My name is Ford. People call me Fordy."

"I still don't—"

"Fordy! Four Ds!"

"Ah, I see. You must get asked that all the time."

"Not really."

Well, that went surprisingly well.

"Do you want to buy anything?" he said.

"No, I just wanted—"

"If you're not buying, the door's behind you."

Good looks and charm. This guy had it all.

"I'm a private investigator, and I—"

"I don't care if you're the queen of the fairies with a cherry on top. If you aren't buying, you can do one."

"I *am* buying." A change of tack was called for. "I'm *definitely* here to buy trophies. Lots of them."

He snorted something under his breath as I began to walk up and down the rows of shelves. They were full of trophies—most of them covered in dust. I was on the point of calling it a day when I spotted it.

"I bought it fair and square," he insisted.

"Do you know where this came from?" I held up the trophy.

"What do I care?"

"You should care. It came from the human world. I doubt the police would take kindly to you fencing goods from the other world."

"That's rubbish. How do *you* know where it came from?"

"I know because the last time I saw this trophy, it was on top of a filing cabinet in my office in Washbridge. Heard of Washbridge?"

"Nah." Much of his confidence seemed to have drained away.

"Well, I'll give you a clue. It isn't in Candlefield."

"It's not my fault. I bought it in good faith."

"We'll see if the police agree."

"Wait! There's no need to involve the police. Take it! Take it and go."

"Oh, I'm going to take it all right, but first you're going to tell me who sold it to you."

Mrs V almost squeezed the life out of me when I placed the trophy on her desk.

"Where did you find it? Thank you! Thank you so much!"

"One of my contacts tracked it down. I'm afraid the thieves removed the plaque from the base, so you'll have to get a new one fitted and have the winner's names engraved again."

"That's not a problem. As long as I have the trophy. It's one-of-a-kind."

That was true. The trophy had been commissioned specially for the knitting competition. Its unusual shape had made it easy to identify.

"Any news on Blinky?" Mrs V asked.

There was plenty of news on that little monster—none of which I intended to share with Mrs V.

"I'm afraid not. I think he must have run away when the burglars stole the trophy."

"I hope the little darling is all right."

"Me too." The 'little darling' wouldn't be all right when I got my hands on him.

"Don't be mad at me," Kathy said.

Her kids were at school and she'd begged me to meet her for coffee. I should have known she'd have some ulterior motive.

"What have you done now?" I said.

"It's for a good cause."

"What have you done?"

"You probably won't win anyway."

"Kathy! Tell me what you've done." Was there some kind of legal immunity for murdering a sibling? "If you don't tell me right now, I promise I *will* kill you."

"Well." She took a long drink of coffee. I swear she was doing it on purpose to build the tension. "You know how WAD has been having a hard time of it lately?"

"Who's Wad?"

"Washbridge Amateur Dramatics of course. Things have been difficult for them — what with the murder."

"Yeah, I can see how that might have been bad for business, but you still haven't told me what this has to do with me."

"Well." She took another drink of coffee. Surely no court in the land would convict me. "They've decided to run a raffle to raise funds for new seating."

They certainly needed it. "You want me to buy a raffle ticket?"

"I've already bought one for you."

"Fair enough. How much do I owe you?"

"Five pounds, but that's not what I wanted to tell you."

"Kathy, you're doing my head in. What are you going on about?"

"The raffle prize. And, before you go off on one, just

remember that your chances of actually winning are remarkably low."

"It's not sky-diving is it? I'm not jumping out of a plane for anyone."

"No, it's not sky-diving."

"Or scuba diving?"

"Nothing like that. It's a date."

"With who?"

"He didn't want to do it either, but they bullied him into it."

"*Who* didn't want to do it?"

That's when the light bulb went on. "No, not—"

"I'm sorry."

"You're kidding."

"You probably won't win. The odds are astronomical."

"It's Maxwell, isn't it?"

"Do you want a top-up?"

I told Kathy that I didn't want the raffle ticket, but she'd already bought it in my name. How many tickets were they likely to have sold? Surely the odds of my name coming out of the hat were very slim. There was nothing for me to worry about. Kathy was the one who should have been worried because if mine was the winning ticket, she'd be a dead woman.

I was still seething when I got back to my flat. As I walked from the car, Mr Ivers tried to waylay me. I didn't bother resorting to magic; I just told him to sling his hook.

Mrs V hadn't let the grass grow under her feet. By the time I arrived at the office the next morning, a new plaque, engraved with all the previous winners, had been fixed onto the base of the trophy. As I walked through the door, she was busy polishing it.

"Looks good, doesn't it?" She smiled.

"Good as new. Are you sure you still want to keep it in the office?"

"Definitely, and I hope you don't mind, but I've arranged for a man to come in later to fit CCTV in here."

"I'm not sure I can run to that kind of expense at the moment. Cash flow isn't great."

"I'm paying," she said. "It's to protect my trophy after all."

"If you're sure. I can give you half?"

"I wouldn't hear of it, and besides I've got something to tell you. I hope you won't be mad."

"Does it involve raffle tickets?"

"Raffle tickets? No. I've asked a few of my friends from the local knitting group to come around later."

"Here? To the office?"

"Yes. I wanted them to see the trophy. Is that okay?"

"Yes. I guess so. Why not? Are you going to introduce them to Winky?"

She shot me a look.

"I'll take that as a 'no' then."

Chapter 13

As far as the police were concerned, the Digby case was closed. The murderer, Harrison Scott, had conveniently killed himself, saving the tax payer the expense of a trial. So how come I was still working the case? A little voice was niggling at me, that's why. While I was prepared to accept that Scott might have had a hand in the murder, I simply couldn't bring myself to believe he'd committed suicide only twenty four hours after I'd seen him.

I had other cases that needed my attention, but I decided to devote one more day to the Digby case. The prop shop owner would probably be back from his holiday, and I had a meeting arranged with Fiona Digby.

'Mastermind' was behind the counter at the prop shop again.

"Hello there," I said.

He clearly didn't remember me, but then he probably struggled to remember his own name most days.

"I called in the other day."

"Right."

"Do you remember you told me you didn't know *nowt* about *owt*?"

"Yeah. I just sell stuff."

"So I recall. Is the proprietor — err — owner in today?"

"Yeah."

"Could you get him?"

"Okay."

It could have been worse. He could have been working with dangerous chemicals.

"I'm Robert Culthorpe." The owner was all tan, teeth

and cheap aftershave, but at least he appeared to have a brain. "How can I help?"

"My name is Jill Gooder. I'm a private investigator. I'm working on the Bruce Digby murder case."

"I read they'd arrested someone for that. Didn't the murderer commit suicide or something?"

"Is there somewhere we can talk in private?"

"Sure." He led me to a small office at the back of the shop.

"I hear you lost your manager," I said.

"Yeah. Stupid lottery. It's left me right in the lurch."

"You still have—" I almost called him 'mastermind.'

"Norman? Like I said, right in the lurch. Norman's my sister's lad."

That explained a lot.

"His heart is in the right place," Culthorpe said. "Just a pity his brain isn't."

I declined the offer of tea—the mugs looked like they hadn't seen a sink this side of the millennium.

"I have biscuits." He offered me the tin—a mix of custard creams and digestives. Tragic.

"No thanks. Have the police been to see you?"

"No, but while I was on holiday, I got a call from them to say they wanted to talk to me when I got back. Then I got another call from them to cancel. I assumed that was because they had their man."

"Can you take a look at this, please?" I showed him the photo on my phone. Kathy had emailed it to me shortly after the murder. It had been taken during rehearsals and showed Milly holding the knife aloft. "Does that look familiar?"

"Yeah. We supplied two of those knives."

"Two?"

"They were identical to look at. One fake and one real."

"Didn't ordering *two* knives seem suspicious?"

"Not in the least. It's common to use a fake and a real dagger in a production. Often the real one will be used in a separate scene — perhaps to stab a table or a door. It adds to the realism."

"It sounds dangerous to me. Surely there must be accidents?"

"In all my years in the business, I've never heard of one. And if the papers are to be believed, this was no accident."

"Do you remember who bought them?"

"It was a man. Pretty nondescript."

"Tall? Short? Young? Old? Anything you can give me to go on at all?"

"I do remember one thing about him."

"What's that?"

"He was wearing flip flops and had this horrible, gammy toe. I was eating a pot noodle at the time — it fair turned my stomach."

Despite my initial doubts, everything now pointed towards Harrison Scott. Maybe he'd put on an act when I'd seen him. He was an actor, after all. Perhaps he'd realised it was only a matter of time before the police put two and two together and arrested him.

After what I'd just learned, was there any point in seeing Fiona Digby? What harm could it do? I had a couple of hours to kill first, so I headed back to the office. I could hear the music as soon as I entered the building — Engelbert Humperdinck, if I wasn't mistaken. As I climbed the stairs, I could hear laughter and raised voices.

'A few friends from the knitting club', Mrs V had said. The outer office was standing room only.

"Jill!" Mrs V shouted, as she fought her way across the room. "Come and join us!"

Frank Sinatra began to do it 'his way'.

"We have sandwiches and nibbles." Mrs V beamed.

"Where?"

"Next door, in your office. I hope you don't mind."

"Where's Winky?"

"He's perfectly safe."

"Mrs V, what have you done with him?"

"I had to. He would have eaten all the food."

"Where is he?"

"Bottom drawer of your filing cabinet."

I took a deep breath. I didn't want to make a scene in front of her friends.

As I pulled open the drawer, I braced myself for the inevitable attack.

"Hey! I was sleeping." Winky was curled into a ball.

"I thought you might want to get out."

"Why? I like it in here. It's cosy. Now shut the drawer."

"Can you breathe?"

"Of course I can breathe. Do you think I'm stupid?"

"Sorry." I slid the drawer closed again.

I grabbed a couple of sandwiches, a sausage roll and a handful of crisps. Back in the outer office, some of the women were dancing to 'The Twist'. Mrs V was showing off her trophy while giving them a blow by blow account of her victory.

I managed to snatch a quick word with her before I left. I wanted to remind her to let Winky out before she went home. She promised she would, but for peace of mind I decided I'd better double check on my way home.

The Digby house wasn't huge, but stood it its own grounds surrounded by a high wall.
"Yes?" A female voice came over the gate intercom.
"Jill Gooder, here to see Fiona Digby."
"This is Fiona Digby. Are you the private investigator?"
"That's right."
"I didn't think you'd bother coming. Didn't you hear about Harrison?"
"Yes, but I'd still like a word, if I may."
"Seems like a waste of time."
"It won't take long."
"I suppose you'd better come up then." She sighed.
The buzzer sounded, and the gate began to open slowly. The driveway led to a small courtyard in front of the house. I parked next to a white van with the words 'Gemini Carpet Cleaners' on the side.

Fiona Digby would have been attractive if it wasn't for her jaw line.
"We'll have to use the study. I have tradesmen in the living room." She made the word 'tradesmen' sound like an insult.
She didn't offer me a drink or even ask me to sit down. Her impatience was only too apparent.
"Did you know Harrison Scott well?" I asked.
"Not particularly. I'd met him a few times at the theatre."

"Are you a member of WADS?"

"Me? No. Bruce was the actor in the family."

"How did you and Bruce meet?"

She sighed, obviously irritated by my questions. "At university. We both rowed and were involved with Ents."

"I thought you didn't act."

"There's more to Ents than the thesps you know. Although they wouldn't agree."

I glanced at the line of photographs on the desk. "Is that you?"

She picked it up. "Yes, that's Bruce and I at a rowing competition. He came second in the men's; I came first in the women's."

There was a third person in the photograph.

"Isn't that Brian Hargreaves?"

"Yes. Dear old Brian."

"I met him the other day. He said he thought Harrison had killed your husband."

"He was right then, wasn't he? Now, if there's nothing else."

"Brian told me he was the understudy's understudy."

She smiled for the first time. "Yes, poor old Brian. Nice guy, but a bit of a loser. Bruce didn't have the heart to kick him out of WADS, but he made sure he'd never set foot on stage."

"Do you have any idea why Harrison Scott killed your husband?"

"You're the private investigator. Isn't it obvious? He was jealous. He thought because he'd written the script, that he should take the star role. Jealousy, plain and simple."

"Would someone really kill for a role in a play?"

"It appears so. The male ego is a terrible thing. Now, I really must get on."

Chapter 14

I was en-route to Candlefield. When I'd left Washbridge, the sky had been grey and it had been pouring with rain. As soon as I was within sight of Candlefield, the rain stopped, the clouds cleared, and the sun began to shine. If ever there was an argument for moving there permanently, this was it. I had to focus hard on my destination so that the car would know to deliver me straight to Cuppy C where I'd arranged to meet the twins.

Amber was behind the counter when I walked into the tea room. She saw me, and her face lit up.
"Jill! How are you?"
"Ticking along. I see you've dyed your hair again." It was black—the last time I'd seen her, she'd been blonde.
"We aren't talking about that." She scowled.
"We aren't? Don't you like it?"
"I liked it perfectly fine until—." Her gaze shifted to the table in the far corner of the tea room. "Until she did *that*."
I'd assumed Pearl must be in the cake shop. I hadn't noticed her in the corner, sitting with another woman. And the reason I hadn't noticed her? Because she too had dyed her hair—black.
"She did it on purpose." Amber's voice was much louder now.
Pearl heard her sister, looked up, and saw me. She said a few words to her companion, and then skipped across to join us at the counter.
"Hi, Jill." Pearl gave me a hug. "What lies is *she* telling

you?"

"I'm only telling the truth." Amber huffed. "You copied me again."

"Don't listen to a word she says. *She* copied *me*."

"That's rubbish!"

"It so isn't!"

Oh how I'd missed this. I'd only been in the shop for two minutes, and already the twins were at each other's throats. Their argument bounced back and forth while I tried to remain neutral.

"I thought of it first!" Amber insisted.

"That's rubbish. I had mine done first!" Pearl countered.

I was tempted to turn and run for the hills, but I hadn't come all this way to leave now. I took a deep breath and stepped in between them. "Girls! Please!"

The twins fell silent.

"Thank you."

"Sorry, Jill," Pearl said. "It's her fault."

"Yours more like."

"Enough!" I raised my hands. "Can we call a truce at least until I've gone? Okay?"

Amber nodded.

"Okay?"

Pearl nodded.

I sighed with relief. "Okay. That's better. I hope I didn't drag you away from your friend." I gestured to the woman who Pearl had been sitting with. The woman, who seemed oblivious to the twins' altercation, was making notes in a small notepad. Even though she was seated, I could see she was incredibly tall. The faux leather cat-suit she was wearing showed off her toned body. She had the look of an Amazon.

"Daze won't mind."

"Who?"

"Her name's Daisy Flowers," Amber said in a whisper.

"Daisy Flowers?"

The twins both shushed me and glanced over to see if the woman had heard.

"She doesn't look like a—" I lowered my voice to a whisper. "Daisy Flowers."

"That's her real name," Amber said. "But no one calls her that."

"Not if they enjoy living." Pearl grinned.

"What did you call her?" I asked.

"Daze."

"D A Z E?" I spelled out the name.

The twins nodded.

"Amber, you get us all a drink," Pearl said. "I'll introduce Jill to Daze."

Amber scowled; she didn't appreciate being given orders by her sister. But at least she didn't argue this time.

"Are you sure we should join her?" I said. "She looks as though she's busy." And very scary.

"Come on. It'll be cool."

The woman looked up as we approached—her long black hair framed a beautiful face.

"Daze, this is my cousin, Jill Gooder."

The woman stood, and flashed me a dazzling smile. "Pleased to meet you."

She shook my hand, which felt as though it might disintegrate under her grip.

"The twins have told me a lot about you," she said in a husky voice. "Please sit down."

Pearl and I did as instructed; Amber joined us shortly

after.

"I understand you're a private investigator in the human world," Daze said.

"That's right."

"That must be fascinating. Do you handle human and sup cases?"

The question threw me for a moment. "Only human up to now. At least as far as I'm aware. The twins probably told you that I only recently discovered I'm a witch."

"That must have come as a surprise?"

"Shock more like. I'm still trying to get used to the idea."

"Sounds like you're a fast learner if what your grandma told me is true." She grinned at the twins who managed only empty smiles in return. "I hear you whupped their asses in a test."

"Beginner's luck, I guess."

"I might be able to put some business your way," Daze said. "If you decide to take on sup clients."

"Oh?"

"Daze is a hunter," Amber said.

"Hunter?" I looked to Daze for more information.

"That's what people around here call me, but my official title is Rogue Retriever or RR for short."

The tea room was filling up, but the staff behind the counter seemed to be coping. Everyone who walked into the shop stared at Daze as though she was some kind of local celebrity.

"What's a Rogue Retriever?" I was keen to find out more about this fascinating woman.

"Let me ask you a question," Daze said. "Before you became aware of sups, what did you think of witches, werewolves and vampires?"

"I can't say I'd given them much thought." It was true. Outside of movies and books, I'd never given much thought to any kind of supernatural creature for the simple reason that I didn't believe they existed.

"That's as it should be." Daze glanced around the room, and seemed unfazed by the attention her presence was generating. "Sups are allowed to visit the human world; they're even allowed to live there. But there are rules and protocols that have to be followed. No sup is allowed to do anything that is likely to attract the attention of humans. The vast majority of sups play by the rules, but there's a small number of 'Rogues'.

"So? You *retrieve* them?"

"That's right. I bring them back to Candlefield where they are punished accordingly."

I thought about asking what form that punishment might take, but figured it would probably come under the category of 'you wouldn't want to know'.

"That sounds like a dangerous job."

Daze shrugged.

"Daze is a sup squared," Amber said, and then shrank under Daze's glare.

"I don't like that term," Daze said.

"What does *sup squared* mean?" I was more than a little curious.

Daze sighed as though she'd given this same explanation a thousand times. "I'm a super sup or sup sup for short. Some people—" She looked at Amber, who suddenly discovered something incredibly interesting on the floor. "Some people have taken to abbreviating sup sup to sup squared. It's stupid."

"I agree." Pearl looked pleased to be able to pile in on

her sister.

"You say it too." Amber retaliated.

"I don't!"

"You do!"

"Enough!" Daze said, and immediately the twins fell silent. You didn't argue with Daze.

"So, are you like some kind of super hero?" I asked, but then immediately wished I hadn't.

"Sup sups have a broad range of powers, but I wouldn't use the term 'super hero'."

I was intrigued by the idea of a supernatural super hero whose job it was to chase, capture and bring back rogue sups from the human world. "How do you find out about the Rogues?"

"Usually the authorities here in Candlefield get to hear, and post a bounty for the Rogue's retrieval. That's how I make my living. Occasionally, I'll just stumble across a Rogue."

"Are there other Retrievers?"

"A few. Not many licensed ones though. We tend to keep out of each other's way. Occasionally there'll be more than one of us after the same bounty. That can get a bit messy."

I waited for her to elaborate, but she wasn't forthcoming. "How do you split your time between here and the other world?" I asked instead.

"I spend the majority of my time in the human world. I'm usually only here when I bring back a Rogue or if I'm on holiday." She reached into her pocket, pulled out a card, and handed it to me. Printed on it was the word 'DAZE', and a phone number. "In your line of business you might come across a few Rogues. If you do, just give me a call."

"Sure." I slipped it into my back pocket.

"Anyway." Daze stood up. "I'd better get a move on—I need to check the bounty list before the others beat me to it. Nice to meet you, Jill."

"Likewise."

"Bye, girls."

The twins chirped their goodbyes.

"Have you got a death wish?" Pearl turned on her sister.

"Sup squared?"

"I was only joking."

"You know she hates that. You might as well have called her Daisy."

"She's one scary lady," I interjected in the hope of staving off another argument.

"Yeah. I wouldn't want to be on her wanted list. She can kick some serious ass."

"Has Aunt Lucy talked about my mother's engagement much?" I asked.

"She hasn't mentioned it once," Amber said. "It's as though it isn't happening,"

"She's in denial," Pearl agreed.

"Do you know much about Alberto?"

"Hardly anything. Mum had never mentioned him to us. As far as we can make out, she and your mother both had a soft spot for him, but he blew them both off."

The door to the tea room flew open, and Daze rushed back in. "Pearl!"

Pearl looked like a rabbit caught in the headlights.

"You forgot to give me the cupcake."

Relief washed over Pearl's face. "Sorry. It's behind the

counter. She scurried across the room, picked up the box and handed it to Daze.

"You should have seen your face." Amber laughed once Daze had left. "You were bricking it."

"So would you have been if you'd thought Daze was coming for you."

As I walked back to the car, I took out Daze's business card. She was one impressive woman, and might prove to be a useful ally.

Chapter 15

Have I mentioned that I hated my sister? I didn't really—I loved her to bits, but she did things that drove me totally insane. Like the time she'd set me up on a blind date with a guy who spent all evening picking his nose. And I still hadn't forgiven her for stealing my beanies. Kathy also had a habit of booking tickets for all manner of events without checking with me first. Last time it was that awful amateur dramatics production, this time it was the circus.

"I hate circuses."

"No you don't," Kathy insisted.

"I do. They're all animal poo and sawdust."

"There aren't any animals in this circus. It's just acrobats, and clowns and stuff."

"I hate clowns."

"Oh yeah." She laughed. "I'd forgotten about your clown phobia."

"I do *not* have a clown phobia. They're just boring." I'm terrified of them. No one will ever convince me they aren't evil. There should be some law against them.

"Then why do you always hide behind the sofa whenever they're on TV?"

"That was when I was a kid."

"What about last Christmas when you came over for dinner?"

"I wasn't hiding. I'd dropped something."

"What?"

"I can't remember. A cracker or a mince pie or something festive."

"You're such a liar. Even the kids were laughing at you."

Children could be so cruel.

"There must be someone else who could go with you."

"You promised you'd go if I found the lagoon blue wool, remember? And besides, the kids want you to come.

"Kids!" She shouted at the top of her voice.

"Is it time to go?" Mikey shouted.

"Circus! Circus!" Lizzie chanted.

"Do you want Auntie Jill to come with us?"

"Yes!" They screamed in unison.

I hated my sister.

"There's acrobats!" Mikey said.

"And tightrope walkers," Lizzie said.

"And clowns," Mikey added.

I somehow managed to force a smile. I'd get my revenge on Kathy – just you wait and see.

The travelling circus had set up camp on a small green on the outskirts of Washbridge.

"You have got to be kidding!" My heels sank into the mud as soon as I stepped out of the car.

"You should have worn different shoes, Auntie Jill," Mikey said. "I've got my wellies on."

"I should, shouldn't I?"

"You can borrow these, they're Pete's." Kathy passed me a huge pair of wellingtons, which were three sizes too big for me. I had no choice but to wear them. It was that or try to navigate the quagmire in my heels.

There's nothing to match the aroma of damp sawdust. They should bottle it – Eau de Big Top.

I checked the seat number on my ticket and to my horror saw we were on the front row.

"Yeah, we should get a great view," Kathy laughed. "Of

the clowns."

Evil. There was no other word for it.

The kids loved every second. They screamed, shouted and laughed their way through a variety of acts. I made what I hoped were suitably enthusiastic noises to hide my derision.

"Why have you got your eyes closed?" Lizzie asked when the clowns made an appearance.

"They're not closed," I insisted. "It's the lights. They're a little bright."

"Auntie Jill is scared of clowns," Kathy said.

Lizzie laughed. "Are you?"

"Of course not."

I kept my eyes closed.

"And now, ladies and gentlemen, boys and girls," the ringmaster said. "We come to our final act."

Thank goodness. Freedom was only minutes away.

"Please welcome the Great Marvinos—jugglers extraordinaire!"

Three men wearing red cloaks and gold harem trousers ran into the ring. After a bow, they discarded their cloaks, and began their act.

Throwing balls in the air, and catching them again— what's so clever about that? I could do that when I was a kid, but I didn't go around calling myself 'The Great Jillino'. But then, I couldn't keep six of them in the air or eight or—how on earth did they do that? Swords? Surely not. Chainsaws? That had to be dangerous. I couldn't watch.

"Look Auntie Jill!" Mikey pulled at my sleeve. "They're juggling fire now."

And so they were. The three men were throwing blazing torches to one another. The lights in the Big Top had been dimmed for effect. The accompanying music became more and more dramatic as they increased the number of torches.

The entire crowd seemed to gasp as one when one of the men dropped a torch. Perhaps it was all part of the act? The torch landed on one of the discarded cloaks, and set it alight. From there, everything seemed to happen in slow motion. The flames spread quickly to a rope, which had been used earlier by the high wire act. People began to scream as they realised that one side of the tent was now ablaze. Kathy was frozen with terror. The kids began to cry. Behind us people started to panic.

I reacted instinctively. As soon as I had cast the 'rain' spell, dark clouds appeared above our heads, just below the roof of the tent. Moments later, rain began to pour down, and soon the fire was out. I reversed the spell, and the clouds disappeared.

"Kids!" Kathy shouted. "Take off your boots!" It was too late, they'd already run into the house. Their muddy footprints were all over the hall carpet. "Great! That's all I need."

"It'll be okay."

"Are you kidding? Just look at that mess."

"If you need a carpet cleaner, Fiona Digby can probably recommend one. I saw one at her house when I went to see her the other day."

"What happened at the circus, Jill?" Kathy still looked pale after her scare. "One minute it looked like we were toast, the next—"

"The sprinklers saved us."

"What sprinklers? I didn't see any sprinklers. It looked like rain clouds."

"Inside a tent? Don't be ridiculous. It's the shock — you're upset. Come inside, I'll make you a cup of sweet tea."

The 'rain' spell had saved the day, but Kathy knew something was going on. I'd have to be extra careful in future.

The TV van was double-parked outside my office.

"I'm sorry, you can't come in." A snotty-nosed young woman with acne and an attitude blocked my way at the top of the stairs.

"This is my office."

She looked at me as though I'd just arrived on the simple train. "We're filming an interview."

"With who?"

"It's okay!" Mrs V shouted from inside the office. "Let her in."

'Spotty with attitude' reluctantly stepped aside.

The room was packed with camera men, sound men, and miscellaneous gophers — all of them had been given a scarf to wear. Mrs V was seated. Her trophy was on the desk in front of her.

A smarmy, middle-aged man with a fake tan and even faker hair was standing next to Mrs V — his microphone poised for action. "Do you mind?" He was glaring at me.

"I don't mind. Carry on."

"You're in shot."

And you *should* be shot, but I'm not complaining.

"Sorry."

I went through to my office.

"When will they want me?" Winky said.

"When will *who* want you?"

"The news crew of course. Do I look okay?"

"It's not a horror show they're shooting." Too harsh?

"I work here too. I should be included in the piece. Does my fur look okay?" He licked a few stray hairs.

"I'm sure they'll give you a call when they need you." Don't hold your breath.

"I don't know why they want to interview that old bag. All she ever does is knit."

"Whereas *you*?"

"I channel the spirit of your father."

"Really? I hadn't realised that's what you did. I thought you were just a massive pain in the ass who only ever stopped complaining long enough to destroy my desk."

"I'll ignore that remark. How about some tuna while I'm waiting?"

"Not a good idea."

"Why not?"

"No one wants to interview someone with tuna breath."

"Good thinking."

"What was that all about?" I asked Mrs V once the TV crew had left.

"They have an arts and crafts programme on at the weekend. They're going to feature my win."

"Good for you."

"Make sure you watch it," she said.

I'd rather poke out my eyes with a knitting needle.

"Wouldn't miss it for the world." I lied. "By the way, I'd steer clear of Winky for a while."

"I always do. What's up with him now?"

"He wanted to be on TV."

Mrs V laughed. I could hear Winky hissing in my office. If that cat took it out on my desk again, I'd kill him.

Winky had retired to the bottom drawer of the filing cabinet where he sulked for the rest of the afternoon. I preferred him when he was sulking—it meant I could actually get some work done. I typed 'pathetic looking dog' into the search engine, and was soon viewing page after page of images of suitably morose canines. After I'd picked one which reminded me of Barry, I quickly knocked up a poster that included the number of one of the 'burner' phones I always kept on standby.

"Are you still trying to find Blinky?" Mrs V asked when she saw the pile of posters in my hand.

"Not this time." I put one of the posters on her desk.

"Who's Henry?" She looked puzzled. "I didn't know you had a dog. I didn't think you could have pets at your flat."

"I don't and I can't. Henry doesn't exist—I made him up. Cute though isn't he?"

"I don't understand."

"It's a long story. I'll update you later."

This time, when I put up the posters, I didn't get any of the cruel jibes I'd experienced when I'd been searching for Winky. I guess people love pathetic looking dogs, but not psycho, one-eyed cats.

I'd just put up the last of the posters when my phone rang.

"Just calling to see how you are," Kathy said, but there was something in her voice that told me that there was more to the call than that.

"I'm fine. What's up?"

"Nothing much."

"Kathy?"

"I had intended to tell you last night."

"Tell me what?"

"But what with the fire and everything."

"Please tell me you haven't booked me a ticket for something else."

"Well — not exactly."

"What does 'not exactly' mean?"

"The show must go on," she said with a false laugh.

"What show must go on?"

"WADS. The play resumes its run tonight. All tickets from the — " she hesitated as though trying to find a suitable word, "From the *abandoned* performance are still valid. So, I didn't actually book anything new. You already had a ticket."

"Who's going to play the male lead?" I asked, but then remembered the man with the nervous twitch. The understudy's understudy, Brian Hargreaves to the rescue.

Chapter 16

Ever had a recurring nightmare? Welcome to my world. Having to sit through that awful play once was bad enough, but a second time? Torture — there was no other word for it. I'd tried to persuade Peter that he should take my ticket, and I'd stay in and look after the kids, but he wasn't having it.

"Don't you think it's a little disrespectful of them to continue with the run?" I moaned.

Kathy shrugged. "The committee took a vote, and decided it was what Bruce and Scott would have wanted. The show must go on and all that."

"Have you met Brian Hargreaves?" I said.

"Can't say I have."

"He has a nervous tick."

"What kind of tick?"

"It's hard to describe, but you can't miss it."

"Poor man."

Milly Brown's understudy had stepped into the leading lady's role. Understandably, Milly hadn't felt as though she could continue in the part.

There was an air of nervous anticipation in the theatre. Hushed voices speculated on Brian Hargreaves' debut. I checked the back row only to find there was an empty seat where Jack Maxwell had been for the original performance. That reminded me.

"When do they announce the winner of the raffle from hell?"

"Not long now. I bet you can't wait for your date with Jack."

"The last thing I need right now is a date with Jack

Maxwell. I'd rather have a night out with a shudder of clowns."

"A shudder?"

"An alley of clowns, then."

"You're making these up."

"A *lot* of clowns, then. Is that better?"

"Why do you keep up the pretence of not liking Maxwell? We all know you'd like to go up the—"

"If you mention hills or buckets again, I won't be responsible for my actions. Change the subject."

Kathy pouted. "Okay, if I can't talk about your love life, how about we discuss when you're going to take me to meet your family?"

Out of the frying pan— "You've already met them."

"Only the twins. I want to meet your aunt Lucy and Grandma."

"You don't want to meet Grandma, trust me."

"Of course I do."

"I'll see what I can arrange."

"When?"

Saved by the curtain.

Brian Hargreaves was a revelation. There was no sign of his nervous twitch, and the man could act—I mean *really* act. He brought the part to life in a way Bruce Digby had failed to do. The tension was palpable when they reached the knife scene. To everyone's relief— particularly Brian's—there were no fatalities this time.

When the final curtain fell, the audience stood as one, and gave the cast—especially Brian Hargreaves—a standing ovation.

Kathy grabbed my arm as I was about to make my way

to the exit.

"We have to go backstage."

"Why?" There was a packet of custard creams with my name on it waiting for me back home.

"We have to congratulate Brian. He was amazing."

Zero to hero—that was Brian Hargreaves. Backstage, he was basking in his new found glory. The dressing room, which was the size of a small broom closet, was full of flowers, cards and good luck charms. Brian had even put up a few of his old posters on the wall. While I waited for Kathy to fight her way through to the pocket-sized hero, I studied them, and recognised the photos on one. It was Brian, Bruce and Fiona—from their university days. One headline in particular on the poster caught my eye.

"Okay, we can go now," Kathy said, once she'd made her way back through the crowd.

"Hold on a minute," I said. "I need a quick word with Brian."

Kathy looked suitably confused at my sudden change of heart.

"Great performance, Brian," I said.

"Thanks?" I could tell by his expression that he couldn't remember where he knew me from.

"Jill Gooder. I came to see you about Harrison."

"The private investigator. I remember."

"You were really good tonight."

"Thank you."

"Do you by any chance have a spare copy of the script?"

"There should be one around here somewhere." He glanced around. "There look, on the cupboard. Would

you like me to sign it for you?"
"Sign it? Sure, why not? Thanks."

"A star is born," I said when I rejoined Kathy.
"What have you got there?"
"A copy of the script."
"What do you need that for?"
"I'm thinking of joining WADs."
"You?" She laughed. "On stage?"
"I was in the school play."
"It was a pantomime, and you were the back end of a cow."
"I was the front end."
"I stand corrected. Clearly RADA will be beating a path to your door."

I flicked slowly through the book of spells. It was gratifying to note how many of them I'd already mastered. I'd almost reached the back of the book when I spotted it—'speed read'. The script was almost a hundred pages long, and it would have taken me all night to check it all with a conventional read through. The spell worked a treat, and ten minutes later I'd completed my check and was headed to bed. I'd confirmed my suspicions—now all I had to do was to get my hands on the suicide note.

I was just about to switch off the bedroom light when my mother's ghost appeared.
"You made me jump!" I screamed.
"Sorry, Jill, I didn't mean to scare you."
"Is everything okay?"

"Yes, I've just been doing some thinking."

That type of sentence never ended well.

"When I marry Alberto, he'll be your step father."

"I guess so."

"It's time you knew about your birth father."

"When did he die?"

She looked surprised by the question. "What makes you think he's dead?"

"At the funeral—your funeral—I asked Aunt Lucy." My mind drifted back to that rainy day; it felt like another lifetime ago. What had Aunt Lucy actually said? I tried to remember. And then it dawned on me—she hadn't actually said anything. When I'd asked about my father, she'd shaken her head. I'd assumed—. "Isn't he dead?"

"I don't know. No one knows. He walked out shortly after I told him I was expecting you, and I haven't seen or heard from him since. For all I know, he could be dead."

"Why did he leave?"

"Your father was a super sup, but he became involved with some very black magic. I tried to stop him, but it became an obsession. The police had started to take an interest when he disappeared."

I simply hadn't seen this coming. After the shock of finding my birth mother, and the revelation that I was a witch, I hadn't given any thought to my father—especially since I'd assumed he was dead.

"What about your wedding?" I asked.

"What about it?"

"If my father is alive, can you still go through with the wedding?"

She laughed. "Of course. My marriage to your father was

annulled years ago. I only came here tonight to set the record straight. Now you know the truth, you can look for your father, if that's what you want to do. Personally, I'd recommend letting sleeping skunks lie, but that isn't my decision to make. If anyone can trace him, you can. That's what you do for a living after all."

I lay awake long after my mother had left. Would I try to trace my father? Did I really want to track down someone who had walked out on me before I was born? Those were decisions for another day.

"Detective Maxwell." I'd caught him on his way into the police station.
"Oh, it's you." He was trying *so* hard to hide his love for me. "What do you want?"
"What makes you think I want anything? I was passing by and thought I'd say 'hello'."
"Hello. Now, what do you want?"
Am I so transparent? "Could I get a look at Harrison Scott's suicide note?"
"Let me think about that for a moment." He put a finger to his chin. "No."
"Why not?"
"Well let's see. Firstly *because,* secondly *because*, and last but not least, *because.*"
"What harm would it do?"
"As far as I'm concerned, you're just another member of the public. I'm not in the habit of showing evidence to the general public. And besides, in case it has escaped your notice, this case is now closed."
"So you'll think about it then?"

"I've thought about it, and the answer is 'no'. If there's nothing else, I have work to do."

"Thanks for your help," I shouted, but he'd already disappeared into the building.

No one could say I hadn't tried to follow procedure, but look where it had got me. The last time I'd needed information from inside the police station had been during the 'Animal' case. On that occasion, I'd used the 'invisible' spell, but I'd nearly been caught out by the spell's time limit. I'd spent several very scary minutes hiding beneath a desk staring at Jack Maxwell's Tweety Pie socks. I didn't want to risk a rerun of that situation.

The spell was called 'doppelgänger'. It was a little unnerving and I would only have one chance to get it right. There were two officers on duty at the front desk. One of them was already busy with a group of three very loud men.

"How can I help you madam?" the young officer said, with absolutely no conviction whatsoever.

"Good morning." I flashed my best smile, and then cast the 'doppelgänger' spell.

"I'd like you to go to the evidence room, pull out the suicide note from the Harrison Scott case, photocopy it, and bring the copy to me. Do you understand?"

With glazed eyes, the police officer nodded. "Yes Sir."

Bingo! That had worked as well as I could have hoped. The spell had caused the police officer to see Jack Maxwell standing in front of him.

The other officer had finished with the three men and was now looking over at me.

"Are you being attended to?"

"Yes, thanks."

This wasn't good. If my officer came back and began to address me as Detective Maxwell, I was in big trouble. I'd never known the front desk so quiet. Where were all the villains when you needed them? I heard footsteps, and saw the door handle turn. As soon as the officer called me Detective Maxwell, the game would be up.

"Someone's nicked my car!" someone behind me shouted.

Thank goodness for car thieves. The other officer forgot all about me, as he tried to calm down the man whose car had been stolen. I thanked my officer for delivering the photocopy of the suicide note, and then got out of there as fast as I could, reversing the spell as I walked out of the door.

Mrs V was all smiles when I walked into the office. "Did you see it?"

I scanned my brain. What was I supposed to have seen? I drew a blank. "See it?"

"Don't tell me you missed it?"

"I might have."

"The arts and crafts show? I told you when it was on."

"I forgot. I'm sorry. How was it?"

"Really good, but there was a little too much of that presenter, and not enough of me and the trophy."

"And not enough cat," Winky shouted.

"Not to worry." Mrs V beamed. "It's repeated tomorrow night."

"Oh good."

"She's changed the cat food," Winky said, as soon as I walked into my office. "She's started buying own-brand rubbish. I can't be expected to eat that. Will you have a word?"

"Yes, in a minute, but first I need you to be quiet while I take a look at this."

I began to study the suicide note.

Chapter 17

"Do you know what time it is?" Kathy sounded half-asleep, but then it was four-thirty in the morning. I'd already been up for half an hour.

"Did you ask Fiona Digby about the carpet cleaner?" I said.

"You rang me at stupid o'clock to ask me about the carpet cleaner?"

Before I could answer, I heard another muffled voice, which I took to be Peter.

"It's Jill," Kathy said.

The muffled voice said something else that I couldn't make out.

"Pete says go to sleep. Goodnight."

"Kathy! Wait! This is important."

"Goodnight, Jill."

The line was dead. My finger hovered over the 'Last Number' button, but if I knew Kathy, she'd have already switched off her phone. If I could only remember the name on the carpet cleaner's van. I'd even checked the book of spells to see if there was one that might help me to remember, but I'd drawn a blank. Oh well, if magic couldn't help, I'd have to revert to old-school methods. There were five pages full of carpet cleaners in the Yellow Pages: a few large display ads, and dozens of small listings. I had hoped I'd recognise the name as soon as I saw it, but I went through the listings twice, and nothing rang a bell. I threw the directory onto the floor, got dressed, and prepared to make myself even more unpopular.

Kathy's hair was a disaster even for bed-hair. She had one eye open—barely, and was wearing what looked like a pair of Peter's pyjamas.

"You have got to be kidding me," she slurred, as she hung onto the door.

"Are you going to let me in?"

"No. Go home."

I wedged my foot in the doorway to prevent her shutting the door.

"It's the middle of the night," she complained.

"It's five-thirty."

"Yeah. Middle of the night."

"It's important, Kathy."

She breathed a sigh of resignation. "You can make me a coffee," she said in a whisper. "And don't make a noise because if you wake the kids, I *will* kill you."

By the time she was half-way down her coffee, she'd begun to take on the appearance of a human being—if you ignored the hair.

"Did you get the name of the carpet cleaner from Fiona Digby?" I asked.

"Seriously? That's why you dragged me out of bed at this hour?"

"It's really important. Life or death." Okay, maybe a little melodramatic.

"What did you spill?" she said.

"I haven't spilled anything. I just need the name of the carpet cleaner."

"You're getting seriously weird, Jill. I mean even weirder than you used to be. It's ever since you found that new family. What's going on?"

"I just need the name of the carpet cleaner."

"I don't have it. I didn't need to call in the professionals. I cleaned the carpet myself. Besides, it would have cost a fortune."

Foiled again. I cringed as Kathy took a custard cream out of the biscuit tin, and dunked it in her coffee.

"Will you call Fiona Digby anyway?"

"What for?"

"Tell her you need a carpet cleaner, and ask if she can recommend one."

"But I don't need one."

"I know."

"It's too early for this. My head's spinning. You're going to have to tell me what's going on."

For the next fifteen minutes, I gave Kathy the low-down, and when I'd finished, she agreed to make the call.

"Morning." Peter looked and sounded like a grizzly bear.

"Sorry if I woke you." I gave him my best smile.

"This had better be important."

"Life and death," I assured him.

"Jill needs the name of a good carpet cleaner," Kathy added helpfully.

It was rare for me to be in the office before Mrs V. She usually arrived a little after seven even though I'd told her a thousand times that it wasn't necessary to come in so early. As I crossed the road to my office block, I could see the lights burning in the outer office. Surely she hadn't come in even earlier.

It took me several seconds to register exactly what I was seeing. There was an empty wine bottle on the floor. Mrs

V was face down on the desk—fast asleep. Had she been there all night? It certainly looked that way. And what had she done to her hair?

"Mrs V!" I nudged her shoulder.

A groan but no other sign of life.

"Mrs V!" I nudged again—a little harder this time. "Wake up!"

She stirred and sat bolt upright.

"Grandma?" I screamed.

"Jill?"

"Grandma?"

"Why do you keep saying that?" She rubbed her head. "And why did you wake me up?"

"Where's Mrs V?"

Grandma put her head back down on the desk and held out her hand. It was difficult to be sure, but I assumed her crooked finger was pointing at my office.

"This isn't acceptable!" Winky fired at me, as soon as I walked through the door. "She's a disgrace!"

I was too stunned to reply.

"Jill!" Mrs V opened one eye and then closed it again. She was flat out on the leather sofa. On the floor beside her were another empty wine bottle and two glasses.

"What are you going to do about it?" Winky sprang onto my desk. "You should sack her sorry backside."

"What happened here?"

"Some ugly woman, with a boil on her nose, turned up last night."

Harsh but true. I let him continue.

"I think she was looking for you. Anyway, I heard them cackling on about knitting and such, and the next thing I knew, they went out together. Good riddance I thought, but then they turned up again in the middle of the night, smashed off their faces. They were singing—if you could call it that—and dancing. I almost got skewered on a high heel. Then, about two o'clock, they both passed out."

Kathy called me a little after nine. I still wasn't her favourite person, but she'd come through with the carpet cleaners' name. I didn't feel too guilty at having disturbed her sleep—I figured she owed me after dragging me to the theatre and the circus.

Mrs V and Grandma were still out for the count, and looked as though they would be for some time. Winky was driving me insane with his self-righteous complaining. He sensed an opportunity to get rid of his nemesis, and he wasn't going to let it pass. I didn't want to be around when the lush sisters woke up. Grandma was bad enough at the best of times. I couldn't imagine what she'd be like with a hangover. And besides, if I had to listen to one more minute of Winky's moaning, I'd throw him out of the window.

It took all of my charm. What? I can be charming when I want to be. Anyway, it took every ounce of it to persuade the man behind the counter at the carpet cleaners to check which of their operatives had attended the Fiona Digby call-out. From there, I soon caught up with the operator in question. Another dose of charm later and I had the information I needed.

Fiona Digby did not want to know. I buzzed her from the gate, but she refused to let me in. "I've nothing more to say on the matter," she said, and then cut me off. I buzzed a dozen more times, but she continued to ignore me.

I'd memorised, but hadn't yet tried to use the 'levitate' spell. The wall was easily ten feet tall, and I'd never been any good at climbing. As a kid, Kathy had scaled trees with little or no effort. I'd been too scared and way too clumsy. She'd goaded me from high in the branches. Even if I had been able to climb, I didn't like the look of the razor wire on top of the walls and gates that surrounded Fiona Digby's house. Levitation it was then.

I walked to the rear of the property where it was more secluded. After making sure there was no one around, I cast the spell. It felt weird — really weird, as I began to rise off the ground. I'd asked Aunt Lucy if I was able to fly now that I was a witch. Much to my disappointment, it turned out that only the most experienced witches like Grandma could fly, and even then only under very special circumstances. The 'levitation' spell was the closest thing I had to flying. It was a painfully slow process, but eventually I was above the wall. Horizontal movement was much more difficult, and it took all of my concentration to propel myself forward and clear of the wall. Now all I had to do was to lower myself down slowly —

Ouch! I hit the ground with a thud, knocking the wind out of me. My knees and elbows were scuffed, but nothing appeared to be broken. I was such an idiot! The spell offered two ways to descend: The slow, steady one — similar to the way I'd levitated, and the fast, instant one. Guess who'd used the wrong one? If Grandma ever found out, I'd be in detention for a week.

I made my way to the house, and peered through the French windows. There was no sign of Fiona Digby. Keeping close to the wall, I edged my way to the next window. The kitchen was also empty.

"What do you think you're doing?" Fiona Digby appeared at the side of the house. "Get off my property before I call the police!"

"Be my guest. You can tell them how you arranged your husband's murder."

Her face was suddenly red with rage. "Get out! Get out of here now!"

"Did you actually love Harrison or were you just using him?"

"I don't know what you're talking about."

"You aren't going to deny you had an affair with Harrison Scott, are you? I have witnesses."

"It was hardly an affair. Just a silly fling. And who could blame me?"

"Maybe not for having an affair, but murder and conspiracy to murder, that's a whole different ball game."

"You're insane!" She spat the words. "Harrison Scott swapped the knife that killed my husband, and then killed himself because of the guilt."

"That's certainly what you'd like people to think, but it isn't what actually happened is it, Mrs Digby? You killed Harrison Scott."

"Now I know you're crazy. How am I meant to have killed him? He was a mountain of a man. Do you really think I could have thrown him off the cliff? And what about the suicide note?"

"When you told me about your time at university, you

conveniently forgot to mention one of your skills."

For the first time, I thought I saw apprehension register on her face.

I continued. "I've seen one of the posters from back then. You were billed as a hypnotist. That's how you got Harrison to write the suicide note and to walk off the cliff edge."

"That's nonsense. You can't prove any of that."

"Actually I can." I fished the photocopy of the suicide note out of my pocket. "Harrison wrote this—it's in his handwriting, but you dictated it. I've had to suffer his play twice now, and I've read his script. He didn't appear to know the word 'only' existed. He always used the word 'just.' Not once in a one hundred page script did he ever use the word 'only' and yet here," I tapped the note. "Here, in this short note, he uses that word twice."

"That proves nothing." She was trying her best to appear calm, but her voice was wavering.

"By itself, maybe not. But then there's the red clay. When I was here before, you had the carpet cleaners in. I've checked with them, and they confirm that you called them in to remove the red stains from your carpet. It was raining on the day you met Harrison at Moston, so the red path would have coated your feet and the dog's paws."

"All speculation. You can't prove a thing."

"The CCTV says otherwise. It has you arriving in the car park shortly after Harrison, and then leaving shortly after the time of his death," I lied. It was a gamble, but I had to try.

Fiona Digby broke down in tears. "I loved that man

more than life itself. All he ever did was cheat on me. I couldn't bear it any longer."

"Bruce?"

"Of course, Bruce. Do you think I could love someone like Harrison Scott? The man made my skin crawl."

"But you used him anyway?"

"He didn't need much persuading to swap the daggers. He hated Bruce with a passion."

"Why kill Scott?"

"He thought that once Bruce was dead, I'd want to be with him. I told him it was over but he wouldn't accept it. He threatened to go to the police unless I agreed to stay with him. I could never live with a man like that. He had a manky toe."

Chapter 18

"I guess that's another case I've solved for you," I said, trying not to smirk.

We were in the same seats, at the same table, in the same interview room that we'd been in after the 'Animal' case.

"I know you think you're helping, but you aren't," Maxwell said. "That lie about the CCTV could have jeopardised the whole case."

"The case that you had already filed as *complete?*"

"If you had your suspicions, you should have brought them to me."

I laughed. "And you'd have done what exactly?"

"They'd have been processed through the official channels."

"Which is cop-talk for 'do nothing'."

"The law is not some kind of game."

"Just as well or you'd be getting your ass handed to you."

"This is the last time I'm going to tell you to stay out of police business. Stick to following cheating wives."

"Husbands cheat too, you realise?"

"Whatever. Stick to what you know."

Stick to what I know? Cheek! What I knew was that he was on the verge of getting my fist in his face. But then, assaulting a police officer in a police station—probably not a great idea.

"I think we're done here." Maxwell stood up.

I followed him out of the door. "If you're struggling with any more cases and need help, you know where to find me."

"Goodbye Ms Gooder."

As I left the police station, I couldn't help but wonder if Dad would have had a better relationship with Maxwell. Was I so difficult to get along with or was the man simply impossible?

Grandma was nowhere to be seen when I got back to the office. Mrs V was at her desk, but looked like death waiting in line to be warmed up.

"Good afternoon!" I said.

"Not so loud, Jill, please." She was holding her head, and there was a packet of aspirin on the desk. "I'm feeling a little delicate."

"Can't say I'm too surprised. Where is Grandma?"

Mrs V shrugged. "She'd gone when I woke up."

"When exactly *did* you wake up?"

"When that stupid cat decided to sit on my head."

I laughed. "Sorry, that's not funny." Hilarious, more like. If only I'd been there to see it. "What time was that?"

"About an hour ago, I suppose."

"How do you know Grandma anyway?"

"I didn't until yesterday." Mrs V was struggling to keep her eyes open. "She came to see you, and we got talking about knitting. One thing led to another and the next thing I know, I'm waking up with that stupid cat on my head."

"Where did the two of you go?"

"It's a blur. I do remember some bare-chested sailors, . and a boomerang."

"Boomerang?"

"Would it be okay if I went home? I think it would be best if I went to bed."

I helped her downstairs and into a cab.

"Why did you sit on her head?" I asked Winky.

"Her boobs were too uncomfortable."

Gross. Erase image.

"And what exactly is up with that other old gal? She's ugly enough to make milk curdle."

"Do you mind? That's my grandma you're talking about."

"Really? Oh deary me. I have seen your future and it isn't pretty. You'd better break out the anti-ageing cream now."

What a cheek. I checked the mirror—not a wrinkle in sight. What had Grandma looked like at my age? Had she been a looker or had she always been—? *Ugly* seemed such a cruel word.

"You've got to be kidding me!" I took a step back from my desk.

Winky gave me a puzzled look.

I used a ruler to lift them off my chair. Men's white boxers with a picture of a boomerang printed on the crotch. How? Who? It didn't bear thinking about. After dumping them in the bin, I wheeled my chair through to the outer office, and swapped it for Mrs V's.

"Looks like those two old gals are getting more action than you," Winky said.

"Shut it or you'll be next in the bin."

I was still seething as I drove to Candlefield. I wasn't sure what made me angrier, the thought of those boxers or Winky's snide comments. I could get *action* if I wanted it. Any time at all. No problem.

This journey was more than likely going to prove to be a complete waste of time. It was supposed to be my day for a lesson with Grandma, but I had a feeling it would be cancelled, judging by the state she'd been in the night before. If only I could get the image of that boomerang out of my head.

The twins were waiting for me outside Grandma's house.

"We've knocked, but she hasn't answered," Amber said.

"Big surprise," I said under my breath.

"Do you think she's okay?" Pearl sounded concerned.

"I'm sure she's fine." Apart from the hangover to end all hangovers. "It doesn't look like we're going to get a lesson today though."

The door flew open. "And what makes you think that, young lady?" Grandma looked even worse than usual, and that was no mean feat. "Don't just stand there. Come on in, then!" She ushered us inside.

The twins exchanged glances with one another, and then with me. They could sense Grandma wasn't herself.

"If you're feeling a little under the weather?" I said. "We could always postpone today's lesson."

The twins stared at me as though I'd lost my mind, or had some kind of death wish.

Grandma looked at me. "Well, I suppose it wouldn't do any harm."

Yes! Result! Let me out of here.

"After all, you're already a competent witch, aren't you Jill?"

"I guess so." Where was this leading? Nowhere good.

"You guess so?" Her expression changed. "You guess?"

Oh no. What had I said?

"Tell me, Jill. How competent were you when you fell head over broomstick during the 'levitation' spell?"

How did she know about that? Before I could ask, she raised her hand and snapped her fingers. There, above our heads was some kind of thought-bubble. I watched in horror as I saw an image of myself levitating above the wall at Fiona Digby's, and then dropping like a brick on the other side. The twins collapsed in a fit of giggles — but not for long.

"And what are you two laughing at?" Grandma turned her gaze on them.

"Nothing."

"Sorry, Grandma."

"It seems to me," Grandma said, with no trace of a hangover. "All three of you have a lot to learn. Wouldn't you agree?"

We all said, "Yes."

"Sorry, I couldn't hear that."

"Yes, Grandma."

By way of a change, Grandma decided we should go to the Spell-Range. I'd no idea what that was, but was too afraid to ask her, so I interrogated the twins en-route. It turned out that all sups had their own private areas within Candlefield. An area where they could exercise, practise and generally be themselves. There were separate areas for witches and wizards, werewolves, vampires and every other type of sup. It was strictly forbidden for any sup to enter a Range other than their own.

"Do you go to the Spell-Range often?" I asked the twins.

"Not really. It's difficult to find time now we have the

shop," Pearl said.

Grandma huffed. "Lame excuse. The two of you had to be dragged here even before you opened Cuppy Tea."

"Cuppy C," Amber corrected meekly.

"Whatever."

"Jill." Pearl tapped me on the shoulder. "Mum says you should join us all for dinner afterwards."

"Okay, that'll be nice."

"I doubt that," Grandma said. "Not if Lucy is cooking."

"Will you be coming too, Grandma?" Amber asked, with her fingers crossed behind her back.

"Unfortunately yes," Grandma replied. "Your mother insisted. Said she had some kind of important announcement, but wouldn't say what. Do you two have any idea what it might be?"

The twins shook their heads.

"She's probably bought a new pair of glasses or changed her brand of washing powder." Grandma sighed. "You know how excited she gets about that type of stuff."

"The beauty of Spell-Range," Grandma said, "is that you have the freedom to practise more adventurous spells here."

We were inside a walled area, which was at least one-quarter mile square. We'd entered through huge metal gates, which were patrolled by guards. Unlike the rest of Candlefield, where everyone mixed together, the Ranges were restricted to a single class of sup.

There were witches and wizards of all ages—from youngsters not much older than Kathy's kids, to men and women of Grandma's generation. The area was so large that there was plenty of room for each group to do their own thing without disturbing the others. I looked around and recognised some of the spells that were being practised. To my right, a girl, no more than ten years of age, was lifting an anvil above her head—the 'power' spell, no doubt. A boy in his teens was racing at incredible speed around the far corner of the square—the 'faster' spell.

"Are you with us, Jill?" Grandma's voice snapped me back to earth.

"Sorry. I was just watching—"

"Never mind what anyone else is doing. Focus on your own work!"

"Sorry."

"Today we're going to practise the 'grow' spell."

The twins groaned in unison.

"Do you have a problem with that?" Grandma turned on them.

"No, sorry. It's just that—" Pearl began, but then thought better of it.

"Carry on. Spit it out. We all want to hear."

"Yes, spit it out, Pearl." Amber was enjoying her sister's obvious discomfort.

Pearl gave Amber a look, and then turned back to Grandma. "It's just that the 'grow' spell is level one and we've been on level two for some time."

"So, you think you're too good to practise?"

"No. No, that's not what I meant."

"What did you mean, then?"

"Nothing, sorry."

"And you can take that smirk off your face, Amber."

"Sorry."

The 'grow' spell was one I'd memorised, but not yet had

a chance to try out. The theory was that you cast the spell on a plant, bush or sapling to make it grow. That explained why Grandma had walked us over to a section of the Range where there were rows and rows of saplings which must have been planted specifically for that purpose. Behind the saplings were rows of more mature trees of varying sizes, which had presumably been 'grown' by other witches practising the same spell.

Grandma pointed to the saplings. "Let's see what you can do. Remember, the more you focus, the taller the tree will grow." She turned to Pearl. "Seeing as you're so confident, you can go first."

Pearl looked anything but confident when she stepped forward. She raised her hand, closed her eyes and began to cast the spell. Amber, Grandma and me watched as the sapling began to grow. Progress was slow, and by the time Pearl opened her eyes—clearly exhausted—the plant had grown from three feet to approximately seven feet tall. I began to clap, but stopped when Grandma gave me the evil eye.

Amber went next. She seemed less nervous, but much to Pearl's delight could only manage to grow the sapling to six feet in height. Then it was my turn. I was terrified I might forget the spell, and fail to make the sapling grow at all. I closed my eyes, and tried to focus all of my energy.

I hadn't realised how much effort it would take. By the time I opened my eyes, I was completely exhausted. The tree in front of me had to be over twenty feet tall. Amber and Pearl looked at me with wide eyes. Even Grandma seemed surprised, but just said, "Not bad."

"That was brilliant!" Amber whispered.

"Yours is one of the tallest." Pearl pointed to the other trees. She was right; there were only a few others which were taller than mine.

"Amber, Pearl. You two stay here and practise the 'power' spell," Grandma said. "Jill, you come with me."

I glanced at the twins who shrugged. They obviously had no more idea of what was going on than I did.

"Did I do something wrong?" I asked, as I tried to keep up with Grandma.

"No. I just want you to try something a little bit different."

We marched across the Range to the far wall. When I glanced back, I could see Amber and Pearl were taking it in turns to hold an anvil above their heads.

"You won't have seen this spell before," Grandma said, passing me a piece of parchment. "You have thirty seconds to memorise it."

I looked for the spell's name or description, but the parchment contained only a list of images. "What is it?"

"Twenty five seconds left." She was holding her pocket watch.

There were three times as many images than I was accustomed to having to memorise. Although I'd got much better at committing spells to memory, I would never be able to remember all those in such a short time.

"Three, two, one, stop!" Grandma snatched the parchment from my hand.

I still had no idea what the spell was meant to do, and before I could ask, Grandma waved to one of the uniformed staff. The young man hurried over, listened to Grandma's request, and then walked to the large building behind us. Moments later, he reappeared, leading a donkey. After handing the reins to Grandma, he backed away.

"Are you ready?" Grandma asked.

"What am I supposed to do?"

"The spell is called 'transform'. It allows you to turn one animal into a different animal."

She was joking. She had to be joking. This had to be her revenge for my making fun of her hangover.

"What are you waiting for?" she said. She wasn't joking.

"What do you want me to turn it into?" Like it mattered. My chances of changing the donkey into anything other than a donkey were zero.

"How about a frog?"

"A frog?"

"You know. Green, slimy and jumps around a lot."

"You want me to turn the donkey into a — ?"

"Frog, yes. Is there a problem?"

"The spell is more complicated than I'm used to."

"Poor little you. Now are you ready?"

"I guess so."

"When you cast the spell, make sure you focus your mind on the target animal or there's no saying what might happen."

No pressure then.

"Which one is the target?"

"The frog is the target of course; the donkey is the object."

"Got it." This could go horribly wrong. I had little confidence that I could even remember the spell — let alone focus on a frog while I did it. I took a deep breath.

"Go on!" she shouted. "We don't have all day."

In the distance, I could see that Amber and Pearl were no

longer practising. Instead, they were watching me. I began to cast the spell—all of the time trying to focus on a frog.

Moments later, and thoroughly exhausted, I opened my eyes to find a cloud of smoke obscuring the area where the donkey had been standing. As it slowly cleared, I could see a frog, jumping around on the grass.

All around me I could hear people clapping, and a few of them were even cheering. Grandma looked on impassively.

"I did it," I said, feeling quite pleased with myself.

"That's a toad," Grandma said.

Chapter 19

"What's the difference between a toad and a frog?" I whispered to the twins on the walk back to Aunt Lucy's. They shrugged.

"How did it feel?" Pearl could hardly contain her excitement. "The 'transform' spell?"

"Okay, I guess. It was really complicated though."

"No kidding." Amber jumped in. "Do you know what level that is?"

I didn't. I had no idea how the system of levels even operated—I just assumed everything I did was on the bottom rung.

"Level two?"

"Level five!" the twins yelled in unison, drawing a disapproving look from Grandma.

"That's like the second from top level," Amber said in a whisper.

I was stunned. Not so much that I'd almost pulled off the spell, but that Grandma had given me the opportunity to try.

"Most witches never progress beyond level three," Pearl said. "We're stuck on two."

"And probably will be forever," Grandma said. "Unless you take your studies more seriously." She turned her attention to me. "And you shouldn't go getting any grand ideas. A toad isn't a frog. You're still on level one and likely to stay there for some time. Understand?"

"Of course, yes."

"Good. Now let's find out what culinary disaster Lucy has in store for us."

We were almost at Aunt Lucy's when my phone rang. I

didn't recognise the number, but could tell it had originated in Candlefield.

"Is that the private investigator?" It was a man's voice.

"Err—yes. This is Jill Gooder."

"I have some information about the Candlefield Cup."

"What can you tell me about it?"

"I'd prefer not to discuss it on the phone. Could we meet later?"

He refused to give his name, but agreed to meet me in a nearby park that evening.

"All of my favourite girls," Aunt Lucy greeted us at the door. "And you too, Mother."

Grandma pushed past us, and made her way towards the living room.

"I've marked the whiskey bottle," Aunt Lucy called after her. She was braver than me.

"Jill performed the 'transform' spell," Amber gushed.

"You should have seen it." Pearl was equally excited. "She turned a donkey into a frog."

"Toad," I corrected her. "It should have been a frog."

Aunt Lucy looked incredulous. "Level five?"

The twins nodded. "And you should have seen the tree!" Pearl said. "Grandma had us practise the 'grow' spell, and Jill's tree was one of the tallest in the Range."

I was a little embarrassed by all of the attention, so I tried to change the subject. "What's for dinner? I'm starving."

"Three day old rat by the smell of it." Grandma reappeared, whiskey in hand.

"The girls tell me you let Jill take on a level five spell?" Aunt Lucy said.

Grandma shrugged.

"Was that sensible?"

"Probably more sensible than eating whatever it is you're cooking. Now, are we going to stand around here all day or are we going to eat?"

"Dinner won't be ready for another thirty minutes."

Grandma sighed. "I'll have died of starvation by then."

"We can always hope," Aunt Lucy said, under her breath.

"What?" Grandma glared at Aunt Lucy.

"Nothing, Mother. Why don't you go and watch some TV. The arts and crafts channel is running a knitting special today. I need a word with Jill."

I could hear Grandma huffing and puffing, as Aunt Lucy led me into the kitchen where the twins had already taken refuge.

"Girls, I need a few minutes in private with Jill. Go and amuse your grandma."

"Mum? Can't we stay in here?"

"Go! Shoo!"

"Is everything okay?" I asked when they'd left.

"I wanted to apologise for my behaviour," Aunt Lucy said. "The way I acted towards your mother was unacceptable. It was petty and totally unfair."

"You were upset."

"That's no excuse. Alberto was—err." She hesitated. "Well, that was all a very long time ago—another lifetime. I had no right to be jealous, and I certainly had no right to say the things I did."

"Maybe you should tell my mother?"

"I already have. We had a long heart to heart. I apologised, and gave her my blessing."

"So you'll go to the wedding?"

"That's what I wanted to talk to you about. Years ago, we promised each other that if either of us married again, the other would give the bride away."

"And so you should."

"But your mother has already asked you to do it. She doesn't want to upset you by changing her mind."

"I wouldn't be upset." I'd be dancing in the street. "You should do it. Please tell her that I want you to."

"Are you absolutely sure?" My mother had appeared behind me.

"Absolutely. Aunt Lucy should be the one to do it."

"Thank you, Jill. You are a wonderful daughter. It's going to be such a special day."

After my mother had disappeared again, Aunt Lucy said, "Were you okay at the Range? With the 'transform' spell?"

"Fine, yeah."

"No side-effects?"

I shook my head.

"That's good. Moving up levels too quickly can backfire. I'm surprised Grandma encouraged you to do it. But then, she must have thought you were ready."

"What level was my mother?"

"Six, of course. I never did make it past five."

"It was only the one spell, and I messed it up."

"Are you sure it was a toad?"

"I don't really know the difference."

"If I know Grandma, she probably picked a frog deliberately. She could have chosen any animal, but with a frog it was easy for her to claim you'd got it wrong."

"I was just pleased it had worked at all."

"You did well but you still have a lot to learn. Now go and join the others. I have three day old rat to prepare."
Grandma was glued to the TV—watching a knitting show. No wonder she and Mrs V had hit it off so well. The twins were at the table behind her. As soon as I walked in, they put a finger to their lips.
"What's wrong?" I whispered, as I joined them.
"She gets mad if we talk when she's watching TV."
"Who's she?" Grandma said, without taking her gaze from the screen. "The cat's mother?"
Pearl gestured to the window. "Let's go into the garden."
The three of us made our way outside. The back garden was a sun-trap and awash with colour.
"This is beautiful," I said. "Is Aunt Lucy a keen gardener?"
They both laughed. "Mum? She couldn't grow weeds."
"This is all Jethro's handiwork," Amber said.
"Who's Jethro?"
"The gardener." Pearl grinned. "He's a hunk."
"You'd better not let Alan hear you say that," Amber said.
"You fancy him too."
"I don't."
"*Would you like lemonade, Jethro?*" Pearl mimicked her sister.
"I thought he might be thirsty."
"*Would you like a cake, Jethro?*"
"I thought he might be hungry."
"*Why don't you take your shirt off if you're hot, Jethro?*"
"I never said that!"
"You thought it though."

"I did not!"

"You did so!"

The Amber and Pearl show was in full swing.

"It looks like Aunt Lucy and my mother have made up." I managed to interject. "Aunt Lucy will be going to the wedding after all."

"That's great!" Pearl said.

"Now we can buy our outfits without some massive guilt trip. Did she say why she'd had a change of heart?"

"Not really."

Aunt Lucy called us back inside. Grandma had wanted her dinner on a tray, so she could continue watching the TV, but Aunt Lucy had insisted she eat at the table with the rest of us.

"Before I serve dinner," Aunt Lucy began.

"What now, woman?" Grandma tapped the table with her fork impatiently. "A person could starve."

"I'm surprised you're so eager for three day old rat, Mother." Aunt Lucy took a deep breath. "As I was saying before I was interrupted, I have an announcement to make."

It felt as though there should be a drum roll.

"I'll be right back," Aunt Lucy said, as she walked out of the living room.

"What now?" Grandma threw her fork down. "I'm missing my TV programme!"

I heard the front door open, and then another set of footsteps.

"This is Lester." Aunt Lucy had her arm around the waist of a man.

You could have cut the atmosphere with a knife. The

twins' eyes were wide, but that was nothing compared to the expression on Grandma's face.

"Hello, everyone," Lester said. He looked nervous, and I didn't blame him. "I'm pleased to meet you. I've heard a lot about you all."

"Well, that's more than I can say about you!" Grandma fixed his gaze. "Where did you spring from?"

Lester was a wizard, and very tall. His moustache was the strangest I'd ever seen. It curled up on one side, and down on the other.

"I live on the west side of town."

"Do you now?" Grandma hadn't finished with him yet. "And how long have you and Lucy been an item?"

"Mother!" Aunt Lucy intervened. "This is not an inquisition. If you must know, Lester and I met quite some time ago."

"Three days actually," Lester added. Aunt Lucy cringed.

"As long as that, eh?" Grandma said. "And you thought you'd just pop in to say 'hello'. That's nice. Well, hello and goodbye."

"Mother!" Aunt Lucy gave Grandma such a look. "Lester is joining us for dinner." She pulled out a chair for him.

"I hope he likes three day old rat." Grandma began to tap the table with her fork again.

"This is delicious," I said. And it was. Everyone was tucking in—including Grandma—although she still made the odd 'rat' comment in between mouthfuls.

"Thank you, Jill. It's nice to be appreciated," Aunt Lucy said.

"What do you do, Lester?" Pearl asked.

"I'm a designer."

"Really?" Amber helped herself to more potatoes. "What kind of designer?"

"Not clothes, apparently," Grandma said, staring at Lester's blue and green checked shirt.

"Mother!" Aunt Lucy looked as though she wanted to hurl her fork at Grandma.

"I design furniture," Lester said. "Chairs, sofas, wall units, that kind of thing."

"How interesting," Pearl said.

Grandma yawned.

It was apple crumble and custard for dessert. On a scale of nought to delicious, it was an eleven. Even Grandma couldn't find anything bad to say about it.

Afterwards, Grandma excused herself and went home. Lester looked relieved to have survived the baptism of fire. He and Aunt Lucy relaxed in the living room while the twins and I did the washing up.

"Did you know about Lester?" I said.

The twins both shook their heads.

"She never said a thing to us," Amber said. "I think that's terrible."

"Because you'd never keep a secret from her, would you?" I grinned.

At least Amber had the good grace to look embarrassed.

"I think Grandma likes Lester," Pearl said.

I laughed.

"She's not joking." Amber began to run the water.

"Are you both crazy? Didn't you see the way she tore him apart in there? The jibe about his clothes was bad enough, but there really wasn't any need to insult his moustache. Even though it did look a bit weird."

"That's just it," Amber said. "If Grandma hadn't liked him, she'd have totally blanked him. The fact that she spoke to him at all is a good sign."
Obviously I still had a lot to learn about my new family.

I'd chosen the park because I didn't want to meet an anonymous caller in a secluded location. It was still light, and the park was busy. The bench was on the brow of the hill overlooking the lake.
"Pssst!" The bush said. "Pssst!"
"Hello?" I walked over to the bush.
"I'm in here." The voice came from inside the bush.
I peered through the leaves to find a short, funny looking man, looking up at me.
"Did anyone follow you?" he asked.
I glanced around. "I don't think so."
"Sorry for the subterfuge," he said. "I'm Gordy. I didn't want to talk on the phone."
"I understand." I was trying to figure out what kind of sup Gordy was. He wasn't a wizard, werewolf or vampire. "You said you have information about the Candlefield Cup?"
"I'm not sure how useful it'll be to you."
"I have precisely nothing to go on at the moment, so anything you can tell me will help. Why don't you come out and sit on the bench?"
"I'd rather stay here, if you don't mind."
"Okay, no problem." I suddenly sensed that he was a goblin. How I knew that, I had no idea.
"I was near the clubhouse on the day the trophy went missing," he said.
"Have the police interviewed you?"

"No. I don't want to speak to them."

"Why were you there?"

"I can't tell you that, I'm sorry."

"Okay. What *can* you tell me?"

"I was there all of that day and had a perfect view of the clubhouse. During all of that time, I only saw one person enter the building." Gordy hesitated. "You have to promise me that you won't reveal me as your source."

"I promise." Like I had a choice.

"It was Aaron Benway."

"Who's that?"

"He's the wizard team captain. I'm surprised you don't know him."

"I'm kind of new around here. Did you see him take the trophy?"

"No. He went into the building, and then—" Gordy looked around again. "He left."

"Empty handed?"

"Yes."

"So let me make sure I understand this. You saw Aaron Benway go into the building, and then leave empty handed?"

"That's right."

"Well, thank you very much for contacting me." What a waste of time!

"Is there a reward?"

"I'm not sure."

"If there is, make sure you let me know."

"You can bank on it."

Chapter 20

Mrs V was back at her desk and looking decidedly chipper.

"Good morning, Jill," she said. "And how are you on this beautiful day?"

"It's cold, and pouring with rain."

"And all's well with the world."

"Have you been at the wine again?"

She suddenly became more solemn. "I'm so sorry about the other day. I really don't know what possessed me."

I did—Grandma.

"Forget it. Everyone's entitled to a wild night out occasionally." Except me apparently. I have to make do with the amateur dramatics and the circus. "I guess you and Grandma have a lot in common?"

"We do. What that woman doesn't know about knitting isn't worth knowing. You should get her to tutor you. I bet she'd make a wonderful teacher."

If only you knew. "We'll see. I guess it was a pretty wild night then?"

"I can't remember much about it."

"What about the boomerang?"

"Boomerang?"

"Never mind."

"What do you think?" Winky asked.

"About what?"

"Eye patch or no eye patch?"

There were days when I longed for a cat who wanted no more than to meow and rub against my leg. Wasn't it weird enough that we talked to one another at all? Now he was asking me for fashion advice.

"Where on earth did you get an eye patch?" Watching him slip it on and off his eye was beginning to freak me out.

"I bought it online, obviously."

Obviously. Silly of me to ask.

"How else do you think I got it?" He slipped it back on again — it looked kind of cute. "I never get to go anywhere else."

"How did you pay for it?"

"I used your credit card of course."

Naturally. "I didn't realise you could get an eye patch for a cat."

"You can't. That would be stupid."

Totally stupid. What was I thinking?

"It's a child's eye patch. From Childrenseyepatches.com."

Where else?

"So what do you think? Eye patch or no?"

"Do they do it in red?"

My phone rang, but when I pressed 'Answer' there was no one there. It took me a few seconds to realise why the phone was still ringing. It was the 'burner' phone in my bag. Note to self — set a different ringtone when using a 'burner'.

"Hello?" I faked an accent which was a kind of Danish-Welsh hybrid.

"I'm calling about the dog," the man said. "The one on the 'lost' poster."

The bait had been taken. I recognised his voice from our previous encounter.

"Have you found my darling Henry?" I said—all Danish-Welsh like. Eat your heart out WADS.

Just as I expected, he said he'd found my Henry. That was some feat given that said dog did not exist. We arranged a time and place to meet later that day.

"What was that all about?" Winky asked, after I'd ended the call. "And why were you speaking in a Russian accent?"

"That was Danish-Welsh."

"Are you running some kind of kinky chat line now? Is business that bad?"

"If you must know, that was part of an elaborate sting."

"If you say so." He slipped the patch back over his eye. "Red? Do you really think so?"

My ten o'clock appointment arrived ten minutes early.

"Do you find women?" The lenses in the man's glasses were so thick that his eyes looked too wide for his head.

"Yes. That is one of the services we provide." Every now and then, I liked to throw in the words 'our' and 'we'. I felt like it gave the agency a more professional feel.

"Is that cat wearing an eye patch?"

"Yes, he is," I said as nonchalantly as possible. "Do you think it suits him?"

"He's a cat."

Good point. "So the woman you'd like me to find? Wife? Girlfriend?"

"Girlfriend. Definitely girlfriend."

"Okay. Let me take a few notes."

I eventually found a notepad under the bag of cat litter. See what I meant about 'professional'?

"Name?" I said.

"Name?" He looked confused. This was going to be a long day.

"The woman's name?"

He obviously hadn't anticipated this level of interrogation, so he had to think for a moment.

"Angelina."

"And can you describe her? Hair?"

"Long. Blonde."

"Okay. Build?"

"Tall. Six feet at least."

The man was five-seven tops.

"And slim, but curvy."

"Slim, but curvy? When did you last see Angelina?"

I could tell by his expression that I'd managed to confuse him again, so I had another go. "When was the last time you saw your girlfriend?"

"I don't have one."

"You don't have one what?"

"A girlfriend. That's why I'm here."

Had I done something in a previous life to deserve this?

"When you asked if I found women, you weren't talking about someone you already know who has gone missing, were you?"

He shook his head.

"You want me to find a girlfriend for you, don't you?"

He nodded.

"That would be a dating agency. This is a private investigation agency."

"Oh." He looked crestfallen. "So you can't help then?"

"He wasn't here very long," Mrs V commented, after the young man had left.

"Do you remember that chat we had a few weeks ago about screening potential clients?"

"I do. It was very interesting. I made notes."

"I think we may have to have a refresher session."

"Shall I find my notes from last time?"

"Not right now. I have to pop out in a few minutes. We'll do it later."

"OK, dear. I'll look forward to that."

I tried to ignore Winky, who was still playing around with his eye patch, as I called the number on the business card.

"Hello?" She answered on the first ring.

"Daze? It's Jill. Amber and Pearl's cousin."

"I remember who you are." She laughed. "My memory isn't that bad."

"Sorry. I have something which I think might interest you."

"Okay. Why don't we meet up and discuss it over coffee?"

"I'm in Washbridge."

"So am I."

"I've actually arranged to meet my sister in a few minutes."

"How about lunch then?"

"Sounds good."

Kathy was at our usual table. "You're late!"

"Sorry. I had a time-waster this morning. He thought I was running a dating agency."

"As if." She laughed. "You can't even get yourself a date."

"Thanks for that."

"Talking of dates." She grinned. "I have good news for you."

"The answer's no. I don't care who he is, I don't want to meet him. I'm done with your blind dates."

She sat back in her seat and grinned even more.

"What have you done?" She had me worried now.

"Guess who the lucky winner of the WADS raffle is."

Life could not possibly be so cruel. "You've got to be kidding!"

"Congratulations."

"No. This is a joke."

"No joke." She was enjoying this way too much. "Jack and Jill are going on a date."

"You rigged it."

"How could I rig it? I had nothing to do with it."

"I can't."

"You have no choice."

"I hate him almost as much as he hates me."

"You're going even if I have to drag you there myself. Think of it as an opportunity to bury the hatchet—"

"In his head?"

"If the two of you can iron out your differences, you might at least end up with a better working relationship."

"You could go in my place."

"I'm married in case you've forgotten."

"How long does it take to get a divorce?"

I ordered a second slice of Victoria sponge. After that body blow, I needed it.

We sat in silence for the next few minutes. I was still shell shocked.

"My life is over." I managed eventually.

"You're being melodramatic as usual. It won't be that bad. Anyway, what else is happening with you at the moment? I rely on you to liven up my mundane existence."

"I turned a donkey into a frog. Or a toad. I'm not sure which."

"Come on. Haven't you got any juicy news?"

"Mrs V and Grandma had a night on the tiles."

"Mrs V? I didn't think she had it in her."

"Judging by the state she was in the next morning, she doesn't. They were both spark out in my office when I came in to work. There was a pair of men's boxers on my chair."

"Whose were they?"

"I've no idea. Mrs V said something about sailors."

"It's a bit much when two old spinsters have more of a social life than we do. You and I should have a night out some time."

"Good idea—I know just the night."

"No, no, no. You can't cancel your date with Maxwell. You and I can go out together another night."

Drat, and double drat. Did she have no mercy?

"Anyway?" I said. "How are Peter and the kids?"

Kathy hesitated a moment too long.

"What? Is someone ill?"

"No, nothing like that. It's Mikey. He says he's being bullied."

If there's one thing I couldn't stand it was a bully. "Who by?"

"A boy in his class. I've been to see the teacher, but she

insists that nothing is going on. Mikey says the boy pushes him around whenever the teacher isn't looking."

"What does Peter say?"

"He told Mikey to thump the kid. Idiot! As if that would help."

I checked my watch; I'd lost track of time and was in danger of being late for my lunch meeting with Daze. "Sorry, I have to go. I hope you get things sorted out with Mikey."

"Okay. And if you need me to help you pick out a new outfit for your date with Jackie Boy, just give me a call."

"Don't hold your breath."

It was a stupid thing to do. I'd only taken the shortcut because I was running late. Two of them appeared in front of me in the alleyway, and when I spun around, I found two more behind me. This was déjà vu. The last time I'd been in this situation, there had only been two 'Followers' and I'd needed Aunt Lucy's help to survive. The odds were much worse this time. The hooded figures worked under orders from The Dark One – a mysterious character who wanted me dead.

My instincts took over. I felled the first with a lightning bolt. The second I threw against the wall using the 'power' spell. The final two came charging at me. One was wielding a curved sword. At the crucial moment, I used the 'faster' spell to sidestep the blow. The sword missed me and instead plunged into the skull of his accomplice.

And then there was one. I hadn't used the 'burn' spell in anger, but was confident enough to take a chance. The Follower screamed as flames engulfed him. Seconds later, only ashes remained on the floor where he'd stood. "Pretty impressive." A female voice came from behind me.

I turned around to find Daze leaning against the wall. Her sleek catsuit had been replaced by a fast-food uniform.

"I would have stepped in," she said, "but it looked like you had it under control. What level are you again?"

"One."

"That wasn't the work of a level one witch. Trust me, I've seen my share."

"Thanks. Nice outfit by the way." I could have bitten my tongue off. What was I thinking? She was a sup sup— you didn't insult a sup sup.

She laughed. "Cheek. Not great is it? I spend a lot of time in the human world. My regular outfit doesn't exactly blend in, and besides the extra cash comes in handy."

"You mean you actually work there? It isn't just a disguise?"

"Sure I work there. Where do you think we're going to have lunch? Got to take advantage of the staff discount."

And she wasn't kidding. When she'd suggested lunch, I hadn't expected cordon bleu, but I hadn't anticipated burger and fries either.

"Ketchup?" Daze offered.

"No thanks. I'm good."

"So fill me in on this case you think I'll be interested in." She dipped one of her fries into the ketchup. Gross!

I told her about my make-believe dog, Henry, the phone call, and my suspicions.

"Don't you want those?" Daze was eyeing my fries. I'd only managed to eat a handful.

"I'm not really hungry. I've just eaten two pieces of Victoria sponge."

"You were right to call me." She finished off the last of the fries. "Where and when have you arranged to meet them?"

Chapter 21

Daze had to get back to her fast-food job. If everything went according to plan, I intended to meet up with her again later that afternoon. I had some time on my hands, so decided to hit the shops. I know what you're thinking, but I wasn't buying a new dress because I had a 'date' with Maxwell. The timing was entirely coincidental. It just so happened that my wardrobe was ready for refreshing. I didn't give a flying fig what he thought of me, and I certainly wasn't going to go out of my way to impress him. What? It's the truth. I swear on a packet of custard creams.

This could *not* be happening! The zip was stuck. I couldn't pull it up or down. I'd only just managed to squeeze into the little black number, which obviously had the wrong size-label. Either that or I'd gone through more custard creams than I thought this month. The dress wouldn't slide down or up—it was well and truly stuck. The surly girl on the changing room door had barely been able to summon up enough enthusiasm to ask how many garments I had, let alone crack a smile. I wasn't about to embarrass myself by calling her for help. Hang on a minute; I was a witch wasn't I? Surely I could come up with a spell which would get me out of this situation. The 'power' spell was the first to come to mind. It would probably have done the job, but it could just as easily have ripped out the zip or torn the dress. Then I remembered a spell, which I'd memorised, but hadn't yet had a chance to try out. What did I have to lose? The 'shrink' spell was supposed to make me—

shrink—duh! One nice aspect of the spell was that I could reverse it at any time. Ideal! I'd shrink myself so that the dress would fall off me, and then I'd reverse the spell. What could possibly go wrong?

The shrinking sensation was really weird. It felt as though someone was sucking all of the air out of me. My first mistake was not to realise that my underwear would also fall off me. Whoops! Tiny me was left naked underneath one of my bra cups. My second mistake was not to anticipate that the dress would slide under the changing room door.

"Madam, are you okay?" Surly girl's voice sounded much louder to my tiny ears. Somehow, I had to prevent her from opening the door, so I shouted, "I'm fine." My voice was so tiny; I could barely hear it myself.

"Madam!" She said again. "Can I come in?"

"No please don't come in." I tried to lift the bra, but the under-wiring was too heavy.

"I'm coming in." The door creaked open. "Madam?" I could hear the confusion in her voice—hardly surprising seeing as I'd done a Houdini on her. Suddenly the bra disappeared leaving me in the middle of the changing room floor—one inch tall and butt naked. The girl had gathered up the dress and the rest of my clothes. She obviously hadn't spotted me or she'd have freaked out. Her gigantic feet were only inches from me—one wrong step and I'd be history. I rushed across the cold floor and took refuge in the corner of the cubicle under the seat. The girl was still tutting as she left. I was all alone, naked and one inch tall. What was I supposed to do now? I couldn't reverse the spell because I was naked, and she'd taken all of my clothes. How did I manage to get myself into these situations? I had to find my clothes, reverse the spell, and then get dressed. No problem. Nothing to worry about at all.

I sneezed the world's tiniest sneeze; who knew the floor was so dusty? A few moments later, I'd formulated a plan. Rather than trying to cover the distance to the changing room entrance in one go, I'd do it in stages. Trust me to have chosen the changing room furthest away from the exit. I made a dash for the next cubicle—running naked was not something I'd ever done before—I don't recommend it. I took a few seconds to catch my breath, and then ran again.

I'd made it to the third cubicle—I was half way to the exit. Just then, two young women came charging into the changing rooms and, just my luck, chose the cubicle where I was standing. A handbag hit the ground next to me with such force that the backdraft knocked me off my feet. I slid across the floor on my backside. That hurt!

Phew! I'd made it past the last of the cubicles. The surly, changing room girl was staring at her phone. Behind her, slung over a chair, were my clothes. Could I cast a spell while I was this size? The only way to find out was to try. The 'invisible' spell did the trick. I was now standing next to the chair, immediately behind surly girl. I had to somehow distract her before the 'invisible' spell wore off. "Miss? Miss?" The voice came from the changing rooms. It was one of the giddy girls who had almost flattened me with her handbag. Surly girl groaned, but then set off towards their cubicle.

It was now or never. I reversed the 'shrink' spell, grabbed my clothes and slipped into the nearest cubicle.

I've never dressed so quickly. As I rushed out, I caught a glimpse of surly girl, staring at me—her face was a picture.

The address turned out to be a small terraced house in the back-end of nowhere. I checked my watch—I was dead on time. After the escapade with the zip, I'd gone to a different shop where I'd bought a cheap hat and sunglasses. Even my own sister wouldn't have recognised me in those.

He answered on the first knock.

"I've come about Henry," I said in my Danish-Welsh accent.

"Are you Russian?"

"No."

"You sound Russian. Never mind. Come in." The man beckoned me inside.

"I've missed Henry so much," I was giving my performance everything. "Where did you find him?"

"He was wandering the streets, poor little lad."

"Thank you for taking him in."

"Think nothing of it. Follow me, he's through here."

The man led the way into a sparsely furnished room at the back of the house. 'Henry' bounded forward to greet me on cue.

"Henry! Where have you been?"

The dog was bouncing around, his tail wagging frantically.

"Or should I call you Blinky?" I said, as I removed my hat and glasses.

The man stared at me. The dog stopped bouncing around; its tail was no longer wagging.

"I have to say. You make a better dog than you did a cat."

Henry transformed into a man right in front of my eyes. He quickly grabbed a table cloth and wrapped it around himself.

"Quite a scam you have going on here," I said.

"We have to get rid of her," Henry said to his sidekick.

The door exploded in a million splinters. The two men barely had time to turn their heads before the chain-link netting engulfed them. Moments later they'd disappeared.

Daze picked up the empty net, which shrank in size as she pushed it into one of the pockets in her belt. She looked so much better in the catsuit than she had in the fast food uniform.

"What happened to them?" I asked.

"They're in a holding cell in Candlefield awaiting charges."

"That's a neat piece of kit."

"The net? Yeah, I had it specially designed. I used to have to transport the Rogues back in person. It was such a waste of time and resources. This way I just have to get them into the net and then BINGO."

"What happens now?"

"I go back to Candlefield and process those two low-lifes. Do you want to come?"

"Sure, I'll have to get my car."

"No need. Grab my hand."

"I did as she said. "How does this—?"

"—work?" We were standing next to a cell. Behind the bars were Henry and his sidekick. Neither of them looked happy.

"There's been a misunderstanding," Henry protested.

"You'll get your day in court." Daze gestured for me to follow her.

In the office, she completed all of the necessary paperwork. Henry and his sidekick had been running the same scam for some considerable time. It worked something like this: The sidekick would look out for posters of missing animals—usually a cat or a dog. Henry, who was a shifter, would transform into the animal based upon the picture on the poster. It was rarely a perfect match, but usually good enough to fool the distraught owner. There had been one or two spectacular failures like the dog which should not have had a docked tail, and of course my wrong-eyed cat. Once Henry was inside the house he'd transform into a man, help himself to all the money and valuables, and then make his getaway. When I'd taken him (Blinky) in, he must have been disappointed to realise that he wasn't going back to a house, but to my office. He'd hung around in the hope that, if he was smarmy enough, Mrs V or I would take pity on him and take him home. When we didn't, he cut his losses and stole the only thing of value—the trophy.

"What's she doing in here?" Maxine Jewell said.

Daze stood up—she towered over the inspector. "She's with me."

"She has no right to be in here, Daze. You know that."

"She caught the two Rogues in cell three."

"Makes no difference. She needs to get out of here right now."

Daze looked as though she wanted to squash Maxine.

"It's okay." I stepped between them. "I'll leave."
"Wait for me outside," Daze said. "I'll take you back to Washbridge when I get out."
"It's okay. I'll go and see the twins while I'm here."
"Are you sure?"
"Yeah. Thanks for your help today. See you around."

"If it isn't our very own *Miss Level Five*," Amber said when I walked into the tea room. "I didn't know you were going to give us a hand today."
"I'm not. I'm here strictly as a customer."
"In that case, what can I get you?"
"Tea and a strawberry cupcake would go down nicely."
No wonder the zip had got stuck.
"You're the talk of the town," Amber said when she joined me at the window table. "No one can remember a level one witch performing a level five spell. Watch out for autograph hunters."
"Where's Pearl?"
"Don't mention her name to me." Amber scowled.
"You two haven't fallen out again, have you?"
"I no longer have a sister. I have officially disowned her."
"That's not going to be easy, seeing as you live and work with one another. What has she done to upset you this time?"
"Upset?" Amber pointed at her face. "This face is more than just upset wouldn't you say? This face is livid!"
"What happened?"
"She's only gone and got engaged."
"To Alan?"
"I suppose so. Who knows with her?"

So bitchy! I almost laughed, but caught myself. Clearly this was not a laughing matter.

"Come on, Amber. Why is that so terrible?"

"She has the same ring as me."

"You mean similar?"

"I mean identical."

"Oh dear. Did she say why she'd chosen the same one?"

"I've already explained a thousand times." Pearl appeared at my side.

"Tell her I'm not speaking to her," Amber said.

Boy was I glad I'd decided to drop by.

"Tell her to stop being a silly cow," Pearl shot back.

I used to think that Kathy and I had a tempestuous relationship, but compared to these two, we were bosom buddies.

"Can I see?" I gestured to Pearl's ring.

It was beautiful, and *very* familiar. Amber was right—the two rings were more or less identical.

"See?" Amber said.

"They *are* similar," I said, as diplomatically as I could.

"It's okay, Jill I know they're identical." Pearl took back her hand. "But it isn't my fault."

"Whose fault is it then?" Amber's cheeks were red with rage. "You're the one wearing the ring!"

"How did it happen?" I asked.

Pearl took a deep breath. "Before the Candlefield Cup incident, William and Alan got along really well. They knew one another long before they met us. Anyhow, you know how stupid men can be."

Didn't I just.

"The two of them had decided to propose to us, and thought it would be a good idea to buy *identical* rings because we're *identical* twins. I had no idea they'd done it, until Alan gave me the ring, and then I didn't have the heart to say anything to him."

"It doesn't sound like it was Pearl's fault," I said to Amber.

"It certainly wasn't mine."

"You know what?" I took hold of their hands. "Men are just plain stupid."

"Hear, hear," agreed Pearl.

Even Amber had to crack a smile. "How would they manage without us?"

Crisis averted—for now at least. If I ever got tired of being a P.I., I should do just fine in the mediation service. "Are you both going to tell Aunt Lucy that you're engaged now?"

"We already have," Amber said.

"What did she say?"

"She took it really well." Pearl looked relieved.

"So you were both worrying about nothing?"

"Looks that way, but I think we have Lester to thank. Now Mum's all loved up, she's not so uptight about us."

Chapter 22

If I had to list my top ten dislikes, karaoke would be right up there alongside Eccles cakes, ponchos and clowns. There were only so many times I could bear to hear the same old songs being crucified.

"You have to come!" Pearl insisted. "It's great isn't it Amber?"

"Yeah, we won't take 'no' for an answer."

I think I liked it better when they weren't talking to one another. "I hate karaoke."

"There'll be prizes."

"Champagne for the winner," Amber bubbled.

"You don't want me there, playing gooseberry."

"Don't be daft. The guys both love you." Amber said. "Say you'll come."

The karaoke competition was a regular monthly event which apparently the twins never missed. Their fiancés, Alan and William, were going to be there too. The rivalry between the two couples was every bit as fierce as you might imagine.

"If I do go, I'm not going to sing."

"You have to. It'll be fun."

Fun in the same way as having a root canal is fun. "I'll only come if you agree I don't have to get up and sing. Deal?"

Amber and Pearl nodded, but I wasn't sure that I trusted them.

The twins insisted we clock off early, so they could take me clothes shopping for something to wear at the karaoke. Thankfully, this time I managed to avoid any zip-related incidents. I came back the proud owner of a beautiful, halter-neck blue dress. It wasn't something I'd have chosen for myself, but the girls had insisted I try it on. It turned out they were right.

"You can come with us," Amber said, her arm through William's. His car was a sporty blue number with alloy wheels.
"She's coming with us." Pearl was hand in hand with Alan. He owned a sports car too — red with a soft top.
Whichever one I chose, I was going to upset the other one.
Just then, a black 4x4 pulled up across the road. The window slid down, and a familiar face smiled at me.
"Need a lift?"
"Looks like I have my own transport," I told the twins, as I made my way across the road.
"I heard you were in town," Drake said. "Thought I'd pop over on the off-chance. Looks like I got here just in time."
"You might regret it when you know where we're headed."
"That sounds ominous."
"Karaoke."
"I love karaoke."
"You do *not*."
"Honestly, it's one of my favourite things."
"You've just gone way down in my estimation. And to think I had you down as classy."
"Follow us," Amber called.
"You heard the lady." I climbed in next to Drake.

The best thing about Club Destiny was the neon sign outside. The lights on some of the letters were out, so the sign now read 'Club tiny' which was actually quite appropriate because there was hardly enough room to swing Winky. The six of us shared a table which was so close to one of the speakers that I had to shout to make myself heard.

"Just so you know, I'm not going to be singing," I yelled at Drake.

"Of course you are." He flashed that killer smile of his. "You and I are going to do a duet. We'll show this lot how it's done."

"You haven't heard me sing."

"You'll be great."

After thirty minutes, I still hadn't recognised a single song. On karaoke nights, you can normally guarantee that certain classics will make an appearance, but the sup world appeared to have its own music biosphere.

Pearl and Alan were the first up from our table. He had a powerful voice and could carry a tune. Pearl — not so much. Amber and William were up next. Once again, the male half of the duo was let down by his partner. If the two guys had partnered with one another, they'd have won hands down.

"Our turn." Drake grabbed my hand, and dragged me onto the stage. As I didn't recognise any of the songs on offer, I allowed him to choose. The song had a country and western feel about it — not my kind of thing at all, but it was too late to bale now. Thirty seconds into the song, he put his arm around my shoulder. It felt kind of nice, but I was sure he'd only done it by way of encouragement.

When we'd finished, I was all set to duck out of the way of flying tomatoes, but to my surprise, we received a huge round of applause. Amber, Pearl and the boys were on their feet, clapping and whistling.

"That was fantastic." Amber gave me a hug.

"You'll win for sure," Pearl said. "There can't be many more to go."

"If we win," Drake said, "the champagne is on us."

The MC took the stage, and announced that there was one more couple to perform. "Please welcome to the stage, the two Ls, Lucy and Lester."

From a table somewhere at the back of the room, Aunt Lucy and Lester made their way to the stage.

"Mum?" Amber looked agog.

"She never comes here," Pearl said. "She said karaoke was stupid."

"Watch and learn," Aunt Lucy said, as she walked by our table.

Within a few bars, Drake and I had kissed goodbye to the champagne. The two Ls delivered a ballad which was pitch-perfect. When they'd finished, everyone in the room was on their feet.

"I didn't know Mum could sing," Amber said.

"Maybe she'll share the champagne with us," Pearl said.

Aunt Lucy lifted the bottle, turned to our table, and shouted, "Sorry, girls. This is all for me and Lester."

"Charming!" Pearl exchanged a glance with her sister.

"Selfish." Amber pouted. "I preferred it when she stayed at home and did our laundry."

"I blame Lester," Pearl said.

Drake touched my arm. "Want to get out of here?"

I nodded. "We're going to shoot off," I told the twins who were still moaning about their mother and her new man.

On the way home, we picked up pizza from a takeaway, and parked on a hill overlooking the park.

"Thank you for tonight," I said, dropping crumbs down my new dress. "I enjoyed it."

"Me too. It's a pity we didn't win the champagne though."

Every time Drake smiled, I imagined what it might be like to kiss those gorgeous lips. I wondered again if tonight qualified as a date.

"Champagne is overrated," I said. "Ginger beer all the way." We clinked our cans together.

"I've been hearing rumours about you," he said, suddenly serious.

"What kind of rumours?"

"Let's just say they relate to a donkey and a frog."

"It was a toad."

"A toad?" He laughed. "Sorry, I stand corrected."

"How did you hear about that?"

"I don't think you realise what a big deal it is. Every class of sup has its own hierarchy. It's rare for any sup to rise through the ranks other than one level at a time."

"I'm still on level one."

"From what I hear, the spell you cast was several levels above that."

"I messed it up."

"People will be watching you, Jill. And not just the witches and wizards. You'll be under the spotlight."

Great—just what I needed.

After we'd finished eating, Drake drove me back to the twins' place.

"Thank you for a lovely evening," I said as I made to get out of the car. Would he kiss me?

"Thank *you*. I've had fun. I'm still planning on coming over to the human world soon. We'll have dinner." That killer smile again. Those gorgeous lips. But no kiss.

"I'd like that. Preferably somewhere with no karaoke." I waved as he drove away. Maybe it hadn't been an actual 'date' after all.

Barry almost knocked me off my feet as I walked through the door.

"Jill! Where have you been? Let's go for a walk."

"It's late."

"Please, oh please."

"Okay then, but just around the block."

"Yay! Come on then, let's go. I love to walk."

Barry was pulling on the lead, but I daren't let him off for fear I'd spend the rest of the night chasing after him. As we walked, my thoughts went to Drake. I was so confused. He seemed keen to be with me, and yet he showed no sign of wanting to take it any further. Perhaps things moved more slowly in the sup world. And, maybe that was no bad thing—my so-called love life had been a complete train wreck in the human world.

The next morning I was stranded. When I'd refused Daze's offer of a 'lift' back to Washbridge, it hadn't occurred to me that I'd be stuck in Candlefield without my car. Twenty miles was a long walk—too long. The twins had been up and out early doors to open the shop. How did they do it? I would still have been asleep if some kind soul hadn't opened the door and allowed Barry to jump on my bed. I'm sure the twins thought it was hilarious.

I couldn't ask Drake for a lift because: 'A' - I didn't know where he lived, 'B' - I didn't have his phone number, and 'C' - he was probably busy. Not that I even knew what he did for a living. In fact, I didn't know much about the man at all except that he had a killer smile, great lips and dark blue eyes to die for. None of which would get me back to Washbridge.

Aunt Lucy would know what to do, but her front door was locked. I knocked twice, but there was no reply. Maybe she was out with Lester. Maybe she was *still* out with Lester. How come every female member of my new family was loved-up except me? The twins were both engaged, and now Aunt Lucy was with Lester. Even my mother had found herself a man. It was coming to something when a ghost had a better love life than me.

Grandma appeared at my side. "If you're looking for Lucy, she's with Fester."

"Lester."

"If you say so."

"I don't suppose you know when she'll be back?"

"She doesn't tell me anything. I'm only her mother after all. She'd promised to see to my bunions this morning."

Luckily, I'd already had breakfast because the mental image was vomit-inducing.

"Do you know anything about bunions?" she asked.

"Me? No. I have a phobia."

"Of bunions?"

"Of feet. I can't bear to look at them. Ever."

"That's what comes of spending so much time living among humans. I suppose I'll just have to attend to my own podiatry." She turned back to her house.

"Grandma!"

"What now?"

"It's a bit embarrassing."

"More embarrassing than falling over a wall?"

"I'm kind of stranded. I need to get back to Washbridge, but I don't have my car."

"It's twenty miles that way." She pointed a crooked finger.

"Yes I know, but I wondered if you knew someone who might give me a lift?"

"No."

"When you visited Mrs V, how did you travel there?"

"I cast a spell. What do you think? Unicycle?"

"Could you cast a spell to send me back there?"

"This is all very bothersome. Where is your car, anyway?"

I told her about the Rogues I'd helped to bring to justice, and how Daze had transported me to Candlefield.

"Daisy Flowers, huh?"

"She doesn't like anyone to call her that."

Grandma fixed me with *that* gaze.

"But I'm sure she'd make an exception for you."

"I knew her father. Handsome man, but had a terrible lisp. Does she still wear that awful onesie?"

"It's a catsuit."

"It's a wonder she doesn't catch her death."

"So, can you help?"

"Do you know how painful a bunion can be?"

"Not really."

"Just pray you never find out." She sighed. "I can't transport you back, but you can try to do it yourself if you like. It's a level three spell, so if you mess up like you did with the toad, goodness knows where you might end up."

I didn't like the sound of that, but then I didn't like the idea of a twenty mile walk either.

"I'll give it a go."

"Give it a go?"

"I mean, I'll give it my all. I'll do my best. I'd like to try — please."

When I saw the list of images I'd need to memorise, I began to wonder if the twenty mile hike might not have been the better option. But then, I didn't want to end up with bunions.

"Concentrate," Grandma said. "If you get this wrong you could end up anywhere in the human world. Or worse."

"Worse?"

"There have been a few cases of the 'split'."

"What's that?" Did I really want to know?

"The head ends up in one place, and the body somewhere else."

Maybe I should settle for bunions.

"Are you ready?" Grandma asked.

"I guess so."

"Off you go then!"

I focussed like I'd never done before. And then I focussed a little more. As soon as the spell was cast, I felt as though I'd been drawn up into a vortex. Would I end up back in Washbridge, and more importantly, would my head still be fixed to my shoulders?

Chapter 23

I landed on my backside with an almighty thud. At least I was still in one piece. It took me a few seconds to realise where I was. It was the smelly, old flat where Daze and I had captured the Rogues. I was back in the exact same spot where I'd left Washbridge.

It occurred to me that I was only a few streets away from Mikey's school. I hated the idea that some kid was making my little nephew's life a misery—maybe I could do something about it. The 'invisible' spell got me inside the school, and it didn't take long to find Mikey's classroom—he was always telling me he was in class 3K. Mikey was sitting in the second row from the front. The teacher asked a question and Mikey's hand shot up. I scanned the room, trying to figure out who the bully might be.

I had only two minutes of invisibility left. At the back of the classroom was a screen, behind which was a small reading area with bookcases and chairs. I slipped behind the screen and crouched down. The kids were all looking towards the front of the room, so I just had to avoid being spotted by the teacher. She was getting the children to contribute ideas for a fairy tale. A girl with pigtails and freckles suggested the story should include a wicked witch. Grandma? The thought never crossed my mind.

Whenever I heard the sound of chalk on the blackboard, I knew the teacher must be facing the other way, so I popped my head out. Every time the teacher's back was turned, the young boy seated directly behind Mikey, leaned forward and pushed him in the back. Once, Mikey turned around and I wondered if he might take Peter's advice and thump the kid. He didn't, and I wasn't sure whether to be relieved or disappointed.

The 'back off' spell was perfect for this situation. Still crouched behind the screen, I focussed on Mikey and the bully, and cast the spell while the teacher was writing on the blackboard. I finished just as he turned to face the kids.

"Aaaarghh!"

"What's wrong, Simon?" the teacher asked.

"I saw a monster," a scared little voice said.

"There are no such things as monsters," the teacher reassured the boy.

"But I saw it!"

"Can you see it now?"

"No."

"Okay then. Let's carry on with our story," the teacher said.

Mission accomplished, I waited until the lesson had ended, cast the 'invisible' spell again, and made my way out of the school. Mikey shouldn't have any more problems. The spell I'd cast would cause the bully to see a monster every time he pushed Mikey. He'd soon learn to keep his hands to himself.

I hadn't yet come to terms with the whole 'time stands still' thing, which meant any time I spent in Candlefield did not affect time in the human world. If I left Washbridge on a Thursday at eight in the morning, spent two days in Candlefield, and then came back to Washbridge, it would still be eight o'clock on Thursday morning. That's why, back at my flat in Washbridge, even though it was almost midnight, I wasn't remotely tired. Hardly surprising considering I'd slept in Candlefield. It was like jet lag, but way more confusing. Having failed to get to sleep, I decided to work my way through the few remaining spells in level one that I had yet to master. When I'd first discovered I was a witch, I'd found the process of learning spells difficult, but now it seemed to come much more easily to me. The fact that Grandma had trusted me enough to allow me to attempt a level five spell had really boosted my confidence. I couldn't wait to move on to the next level.

When I arrived at the office the next morning, Mrs V wasn't at her desk which was most unusual. Maybe she and Grandma had been on another all-nighter. By eleven o'clock, she was still a no-show, and I was beginning to get worried. I tried calling her, but she didn't pick up. I had a bad feeling about this.

I was trying to extract Winky from the window blinds—that cat never learned—when the phone rang. It must be Mrs V.
"Wait there," I said to Winky.
"Like I have a choice."
It was the hospital. Mrs V had asked the nurse to contact me. Apparently she'd had a funny turn in the night and been taken by ambulance to St Meads. The nurse told me that Mrs V was feeling much better this morning, but that they'd be keeping her in for a couple of days to be on the safe side. I could visit at any time, and would I bring her a pair of size nine needles and five balls of

crimson dream wool which I'd find in the linen basket. I'd no sooner hung up, than it rang again.

"Don't mind me," shouted Winky. "I'll just hang on here."

"It's your own fault!"

"What?" Kathy said.

"Not you. I was talking to the cat."

"Have you still got that ugly one-eyed thing?"

"'I'm afraid so. Hey, why don't you adopt him for the kids?"

"Are you joking? That monster would give them nightmares."

"My claws are falling out!" Winky yelled.

"Did you call for something in particular? Only, the cat's stuck in the blind and Mrs V is in hospital."

"Is she okay?"

"Sounds like it. I'm going over there as soon as I get off the phone."

"What about me?" Winky screamed.

"As soon as I get off the phone, *and* free the cat."

"I only rang to remind you about your date with Jack."

"Thanks. Like I could forget."

"Do you need someone to cover for Mrs V while she's in hospital?"

"You?"

"Not me. I've got real work to do. One of my friends is a PA. She's between jobs. She might be able to step in for a few days."

"Okay. Tell her to give me a call. Gotta dash."

Mrs V was sitting up in bed, watching the arts and crafts station on TV. Apart from being a little pale, she looked pretty much herself.

"Did you bring my knitting?"

"Here it is." I passed her the carrier bag. "Size nine needles and five balls of 'crimson dream'."

"You're a life saver. I was going crazy. I've promised the nice doctor that I'll knit him a scarf in his favourite colour."

"What happened to you?"

"It's my own fault. I over did the reps."

"Reps?"

"Repetitions. I usually do five dead lifts, but I went for six."

"Dead lift? Isn't that weight lifting?"

"Yes dear."

"What were you doing weight lifting?"

"I thought I'd told you about it."

"That you did weight lifting? No. I'm pretty sure I'd have remembered that."

"I have my own gym set up in the back bedroom."

"I suppose it makes a change from knitting."

Mrs V wanted to get back to work, but the doctors had insisted she take at least a week off.

"How will you manage without me?" she asked.

"Don't worry. Kathy said she knows someone who can step in."

I stayed with Mrs V for just over an hour. In the end, she told me to leave because she wanted to make a start on the scarf. On the way back to the office, I called in at my favourite diner for a mixed grill. I'd been trying to block out all thoughts of the Maxwell date, but it wasn't easy because it was only a couple of days away now. It might just turn out to be the longest and most painful night of my entire life. I'd rather spend a night as Winky's scratching board.

For a moment, I thought I'd walked into the wrong office. The desk had been moved to the far wall. The linen basket and trophy were nowhere to be seen.

"You must be Jill." The young woman with 'don't mess with me' glasses, and a tight bun, walked over to greet me.

"Hi, and you are?"

"Sue Zann."

"Suzanne, nice to meet you."

"Not Suzanne. Sue Zann."

"Suzanne?"

"No. My first name is Sue, and my last name is Zann. Sue Zann."

"Sue Zann. Right. I suppose you get that a lot. The whole Sue Zann, Suzanne thing."

"Not really."

Just me then. "Did my sister send you?"

"Yes. Kathy said you had a temporary crisis and asked me to help out."

"Thank you. It's much appreciated. Just one thing — well two actually."

"Yes?"

"Where are the linen basket and the trophy?"

"Did you know the basket was full of wool?"

"Yeah. You haven't thrown it away have you?" How would I break it to Mrs V? It would kill her.

"Of course not. It's in the large cupboard on the landing. The trophy is in there too."

Phew. Crisis averted.

"Okay, thanks. I'll leave you to it then."

"One more thing," Sue said. "A cat had got into your office. An ugly, manky old thing with only one eye."

Ugly? Manky?

"I called the cat re-homing centre and had them collect it."

I turned tail and rushed back out the door.

"I'm looking for a cat," I said, still trying to catch my breath.

The woman behind the counter sighed. "Just as well because we're right out of llamas."

A smart ass. Just what I needed.

"Your people collected him from my office earlier today."

She took out a form — there were a lot of boxes on it.

"Name?"

"Winky."

"*Your* name?"

"Sorry. Jill Gooder."

"Name of cat?"

"Winky."

"Winky?"

"Yes."

"Description?"

"Of me or the cat?"

She gave me a stony look.

"He has one eye."

"Anything else?"

"How many one-eyed cats do you have?"

"And you say he was collected from your office this

afternoon. What was he doing there?"

"He lives there."

"In your office?"

"Yes."

"So why ask us to collect him if you still want him?"

"I didn't, it was the temp, Sue Zann."

"Suzanne?"

"No, Sue Zann—never mind. It was a misunderstanding."

"There'll be a charge."

"Of course."

"Then there's the collection fee."

"Right."

"And the accommodation fee."

"Accommodation? He can't have been here for more than a couple of hours."

"Three day minimum."

"Of course."

"And the administration fee."

"What's that for?"

"Filling out this form."

"They threw my eye patch away," Winky said, as I carried him back to the car.

"It didn't suit you anyway."

"Have you got rid of her?"

"Who?"

"That psycho who got me locked up."

"That's Sue Zann. She's going to temp for me while Mrs V is off."

"I don't think so. Have you seen that weird ball of hair on top of her head?"

"That's a bun."

"What is?"

"Her hair is in a bun."

"I don't care. Get rid of her and bring the old bag back."

"The old bag—err, I mean Mrs V is in hospital. She's going to be off for at least a week. Sue Zann will be standing in until she's well enough to come back."

"Well that's just peachy. You'd better keep her away from me then or I won't be responsible for my actions."

Sue Zann had already clocked off and gone home by the time Winky and I arrived back at the office. I placated Winky with a bowl of food and a promise to buy him a red eye patch. I left the desk where it was, but brought the linen basket and trophy back into my office. If someone stole those it would kill Mrs V. And then, her ghost would most probably haunt me.

Before I left, I wrote a note for Sue Zann explaining that Winky was my cat. I considered asking her to feed him in the morning, but decided that was probably over and above a PA's normal duties—to say nothing of dangerous. Winky wasn't one to forgive and forget.

I gave myself a night off from study. I was fairly confident that I'd now mastered all level one spells—Grandma would probably disagree. It was a night for custard creams and ginger beer. Oh, yeah—walking on the wild side.

Every time I walked into the wardrobe, I felt a twinge of sadness. My poor beanies—gone forever. All except the squid of course.

"Sorry little guy," I gave him a cuddle. I felt bad about

having to lock him away in the cupboard, but if I left him out on display, Kathy and Lizzie would stake their claim. If only that mirror wasn't there, I could cast a spell to hide him.

And that's when it struck me.

Chapter 24

"Thank you both for coming here at such short notice," I said, trying to keep my nerves in check.

I was in the clubhouse with the captain of the vampire team, Archie Maine, and the captain of the werewolf team, Wayne Holloway. They were both imposing figures in their own way. Archie was the taller of the two, but Wayne just about edged it on overall physique. They were immaculately dressed in suits. Archie in black, Wayne in charcoal.

"I'm sure I speak for both of us," Wayne said, "when I say it's good to know that someone is actually treating this issue seriously. The local police have so far seemed spectacularly uninterested."

The two men nodded in agreement.

"I'm sure their resources are stretched." Ever the diplomat, that's me. It was much more likely that the Candlefield police were as incompetent as Maxwell and his crew. "One thing that struck me on the first occasion I met you two gentlemen, and again now, is that you seem to get on very well. Maybe you're very good at hiding it, but I don't sense any animosity."

The two men exchanged a smile, and then hesitated as though unsure which of them should respond. Wayne broke the silence. "Archie and I go way back. We've competed in this competition since we were youngsters. On the field, we're opponents, but off the field we have great respect for one another."

As Wayne spoke, Archie nodded his head, and then picked up the thread. "There's no denying this has caused a lot of animosity, but most of it has been among the supporters, and maybe a few of the younger players."

"So neither of you blames the other?"

"I can't speak for Wayne," Archie said. "But all along, my feeling has been that this wasn't perpetrated by anyone connected to the teams. More likely, it's some element wanting to stir up trouble."

"I agree," Wayne nodded.

"Did you say as much to the police?" I asked.

Both men laughed. "We would have, if anyone had asked. The truth is that the police, and Maxine Jewell in particular, see this as a 'nothing' case, which admittedly in the scheme of things it probably is."

"Something else interests me." I was warming to the two men. "How do you feel about the exclusion of the wizards? I understand that the Candlefield Cup used to be a three-way competition at one time."

The question seemed to hit a nerve with both of them. Their smiles disappeared and they looked at one another.

"Do you know the history, Jill?" Wayne asked.

"I know that the wizards were forced to withdraw for a number of years because they were unable to field a team due to a virus."

"That's right. Archie and I had just come into our respective teams at the time, so we never got to compete against the wizards."

There was an uneasy silence, and I felt as though both men were holding back.

"Can it be right to still keep them out?" I asked.

The uneasy silence continued for a few seconds until Wayne broke it. "Speaking for myself, I'd like to see the competition return to a three-way event, but I know Archie would never countenance it."

"Hold on right there," Archie said. "I've long thought the wizards should be allowed to return, but I knew that you would veto such a move."

The two men stared at one another.

"Let me see if I understand this correctly," I said. "Archie, you'd like to return to a three-way competition, but think Wayne would object? And Wayne, you think the same about Archie?"

"It looks that way," Archie said. "But it's a bit more complicated. There are many vampires who would be opposed to the wizards being invited back into the competition."

"Many werewolves too," Wayne said.

"But ultimately, it's your decision. The two of you. Is that correct?"

They nodded.

"I believe the competition is due to take place in a few days' time," I said. "Why not make it a three-way event this year?"

"It's not that easy."

"It's as easy as you want it to be. Be brave gentlemen."

The two men looked at me, and then at one another. I wasn't sure what to expect, but then they smiled.

"Let's do it," Wayne said.

"I hope we know what we're doing." The two men shook hands.

"What's the worst that can happen?"

"We may well find out."

"Now all we need is a trophy to play for," Archie said.

"I might be able to help with that." I'd been biding my

time. "Would you both mind sitting on this side of the table?"

They shared a puzzled expression, but did as I'd asked and sat with their backs to the plinth.

"Ready?" I asked.

"What's going on, Jill?" Archie shuffled in his seat.

I took a small mirror from my bag and held it up in front of them. Their reaction was as one. Open-mouthed they spun around to look at the plinth, and then back at the mirror.

"The cup?" Archie said.

"The cup is behind you—where it's always been. The spell, which is obscuring it from your view, does not prevent its reflection from being seen. That's why the mirror was destroyed at the same time as the spell was cast."

"It's been here all along?" Wayne shook his head in disbelief. "How can we reverse the spell?"

"I could reverse it," I said. "But there's someone else who I think should do it." I walked over to the door, opened it, and in walked Aaron Benway—in his arm was a rectangular parcel wrapped in brown paper.

"Aaron?" Archie gasped.

"Benway, I might have known." Wayne grinned.

This had been the moment I'd been dreading. I wasn't sure how the two men would react once they knew who the culprit was.

"Gentlemen," Aaron nodded to them. "First of all I'd like to apologise for the childish prank. It was borne out of frustration, but even so it isn't something I'm particularly proud of." He looked towards the plinth, and reversed the spell. "I bought you this." He put the parcel on the table. "It's a mirror to replace the one I broke. It's as close a match to the original as I could find. Again, I'm sorry for my actions, but you have to understand the frustration that I, and all my team mates, feel at not being able to compete in the Candlefield Cup."

I had everything crossed. Would the two seated men be so angry that they'd go back on their earlier decision?

You could have cut the tension with a knife. It was Wayne who eventually spoke. "Speaking for myself, I'm not impressed with what you did to the trophy or the mirror." He took a deep breath. "But then, I'm not impressed by the way we've treated your team over the last few years."

"I agree," Archie said. "It took Jill here to make us see how stubborn and ridiculous we've been acting."

"Does that mean you'll allow the wizards to take part from now on?" I asked.

Wayne and Archie looked at one another, and then turned to Aaron.

"Welcome back," Archie said.

The three men shook hands.

I had no idea this was such a big deal," I said.

The Candlefield Cup wasn't just one of the most important sporting events in the Candlefield calendar; it was also a major carnival. All around the stadium, where the competition was to take place, a small village of stalls and funfair rides had sprung up. The beautiful weather had played its part too; it felt as though all Candlefield had turned out.

"The Cup's always been popular; even more so this year,

thanks to you," Aunt Lucy said. "It was never the same without all three teams competing."

"How will all of these people get inside the stadium?"

"They won't. A lot of people come just for the carnival. Not everyone is a fan of BoundBall."

"What about you? Do you like it?" I asked.

"I don't understand it, dear."

"The twins seem keen."

"Don't kid yourself. It's only since they hooked up with William and Alan. Until then, they'd always said they hated it. Now, suddenly they're big fans. Between you and me, I don't think either of them has the first clue how the game works."

I laughed. The twins had shut Cuppy C for the day. It seemed like most of the shops in Candlefield were closed. Everyone was at the carnival.

"I feel guilty about taking a seat when I don't know anything about the game," I said, as I watched someone throwing balls at the coconut shy. "Isn't there someone I could give it to?"

"You have to go. You're the guest of honour."

That made it worse not better. The three team captains had insisted I accept a ticket in the Captains' Box. The twins had been green with envy when they heard.

"Jill!" Speaking of the twins, they appeared from behind the tombola stand. Amber was struggling with a huge stick of candy floss while Pearl's lips were stained red from the toffee apple she was eating.

"Want a bite?" Amber offered her candy floss to me.

"No thanks." I couldn't abide the sickly, sweet cobwebs.

"Where are the guys?" Aunt Lucy asked.

The twins had set out early to meet up with their fiancés,

Alan and William, who would be on opposing sides in the competition.

"They had to join their teams."

"Are they nervous?" I offered Pearl a tissue to wipe her mouth. Her clown impression was freaking me out.

"Alan isn't," Pearl said. "He knows they'll win."

"In his dreams." Amber scoffed. "The werewolves' name is as good as on the cup."

Amber was dressed all in red—the werewolf team's colours. Pearl sported all blue—the vampire team's colours.

"Who will you be cheering for, Jill?" Aunt Lucy asked while taking a tissue to Amber's face.

I'd deliberately avoided dressing in blue, red or green—the colours of the three teams. As I was to be seated in the Captains' Box, I thought I should remain neutral.

"No one. If the witches had a team, I'd cheer for them."

"Witches don't waste their time with BoundBall," Amber said. "It's a game for softies." She glanced around. "Don't tell William I said that. We play PitchOrDie. Now that's a real game."

"PitchOrDie?"

"Don't worry. No one has ever actually died. Not yet anyway. It's way better than BoundBall," Pearl said. "We'll take you to a game some time."

Yay! "That'll be great." I hated all team sports.

With thirty minutes to go until the first game, I left Aunt Lucy and the twins, and made my way to the Captains' Box. Archie, Aaron and Wayne were all there, and greeted me warmly. They each introduced me to their respective vice captain.

"We've already met." Drake grinned.

"I didn't know you played BoundBall," I said.

"Ever since I was a child. And thanks to you, I get to play in my first Candlefield Cup."

A bell rang in the box.

"We'd better get down to the changing room," Drake said. "Maybe I'll see you later."

"Maybe. Good luck—all of you."

The tournament had reverted to its original 'round robin' format where each team played the other two. The team with the most points at the end of the day took the trophy.

I'd like to say I was on the edge of my seat, but I'd be lying. I'd like to say I understood the rules of the game, but I'd be lying again. Luckily, everyone else in the stadium seemed to be having a great time.

Three games and what felt like a lifetime later, we had a winner. I'd been invited to present the trophy to the winning captain. Aaron Benway lifted the cup aloft to huge cheers from the wizard section of the stadium, and polite applause from the rest. After a few seconds, he took the microphone and hushed the crowd.

"Ladies and gentlemen. There are two reasons I am able to hold this trophy aloft today. Firstly because the wizards are clearly the better team." Wizards cheered; everyone else booed good-naturedly. "The second reason is this young woman."

I wanted the ground to open up beneath my feet. Colour flushed my cheeks.

"Jill Gooder was single-handedly responsible for restoring this tournament to its original glory. Let's give her a round of applause."

The whole stadium took to their feet. All eyes seemed to

be on me.

Chapter 25

Mrs V was back at her desk, knitting needles in hand, but she didn't look very happy.

"I'm not happy," she said. See—nothing gets past me. That's why I'm a P.I.

"Someone has jumbled up my yarn."

"I'm sorry about that. The temp I got in was a little over enthusiastic."

She harrumphed. "And what's wrong with that cat?"

"What's he done now?"

"He purred at me, and rubbed against my leg. He's acting friendly."

"He is?"

"He's up to something if you ask me."

"Leave it with me. I'll see to Winky. How are you feeling anyway? Is there anything you need?"

"I feel fine, thanks. I wouldn't say no to a cup of tea though. Two sugars."

Ah, I'd missed this.

"What are you up to?" I asked Winky, who was scratching his ear.

"What does it look like? My ear itches."

"With Mrs V, I mean. What are you plotting?"

"Nothing, I was being nice to her."

"There! That's what I mean. What are you up to?"

"Sheesh. A cat can't win around here. When I'm nasty to her, you complain. Now I'm being nice, you think I'm up to something."

"You don't do nice."

"Don't worry. It won't last long. It's just the relief at

getting rid of the buninator. Don't ever let her come back or I won't be responsible for my actions."

I hadn't seen my mother's ghost for a while, so I was a little startled when she appeared at my desk.

"Hi," I said.

"I'm sorry I haven't been around, but Lucy and I have been so busy with the wedding arrangements. By the way, what do you make of Lester?"

"Hard to say. I haven't seen much of him yet. He has a cracking voice though. He cost me a bottle of champagne."

She laughed. "Yes, I heard all about that. I've also been hearing good things about your progress from Grandma."

"She said I was making progress?"

"Of course not. She said you were doing okay."

"Just okay?"

"Trust me, that's praise indeed from her. And I heard about the donkey."

"I'm trying to forget that."

"You shouldn't. You're doing really well. But that's not the reason I'm here. I wanted to let you know the date of the wedding. Mark it in your diary now—July 23rd. Anyway, I have to rush. I left Alberto in charge of dinner, and you know what men are like in the kitchen."

"But—" It was too late—she'd gone. *Now* what was I supposed to do? July 23rd was Kathy's birthday. We always went out together on our birthdays. We hadn't missed one since Dad died. Even though time in Washbridge stood still while I was in Candlefield, it was still going to be tricky trying to juggle both events.

Somehow though, I'd have to manage it—what was the alternative? I could hardly tell Kathy that my dead mother's ghost was getting married. And, not attending the wedding wasn't an option—it would break my mother's heart—assuming ghosts had hearts. Aunt Lucy and the twins would be upset, and Grandma would probably kill me.

Speaking of whom, Grandma was waiting for me at the door to her house.
"I'm not late am I?"
"Can you tell the time?"
"Yes, it's five to."
"Then you're not late. Go through to the living room."
What was it about Grandma that always made me feel like a naughty child who'd been caught with her fingers in the custard cream jar?
"The twins aren't here yet," I said, when Grandma joined me.
"Nothing wrong with your powers of observation, I see."
"I meant—where are they?"
"I gave them the day off."
What about me? I wanted a day off too. "Oh?"
"Don't pout. It doesn't suit you. Sit down. There's something I want to discuss with you."
This didn't sound good. What had I done now, and what ghastly punishment awaited me?
"Level one."
"Yes?"
"Are you competent in all the spells in level one?"
Was it a trick question? Knowing Grandma, it had to be.

If I said yes, she'd take great pleasure in humiliating me by proving I wasn't. If I said no, she'd want to know why not. "Yes, no, I'm not sure."

"Yes? No? Which is it?"

"Yes, I think I am."

"Only think?"

"I am competent. Definitely." I tried, but failed to sound confident.

"I agree."

Say what? "Pardon?"

"I agree that you are now competent in level one spells — just about. It's time for you to move on to the next level, which even you must be able to work out, is level two. Are you ready for that?"

I nodded. The twins were on level two — they'd be able to help me.

"And don't even think of asking Lucy's girls for help."

She could read my mind. Of course she could. Even I could do that, but she did it so effortlessly. And now, she was reading this too. Bum.

"Those girls have been floundering on level two for way too long. The kind of help they can give you is the kind of help you don't need. Understand?"

"Got it. When will I receive the new spell book?"

"It's waiting for you back at your flat in the human world. It's replaced the one you've been using up until now. I've included with it a list of the first spells I'd like you to learn."

"Thank you."

"What are you waiting for? Off you go."

"Right. Thank you. Bye."

The night I'd been dreading had arrived. Kathy had been taking no chances. She'd come to my flat just after six to make sure I didn't try to pull a fast one. As if I'd pretend to be ill. The thought had never even crossed my mind.
"I really do have stomach ache." I rubbed my tummy.
"No you don't. Now get ready."
"It hurts so bad."
"Nobody cares. Now are you going to get ready or do I have to dress you myself?"
"It'll be a disaster. Maxwell hates me."
"So? The feeling is obviously mutual — you should get on like a house on fire."
"How long do I have to stay?"
"It's a dinner date. You have to stay at least until after the main course. Unless he offers you *afters.*" Kathy grinned.
"Eww. Don't!"
"You can't deny he's hot. You said so yourself."
"That was before I knew him. He's got such an attitude."
"The two of you were obviously made for one another then."
"I do *not* have an attitude."
There she was again with *that* look.
"I don't."

Restaurant Ramon was located in the four-star Hotel Palermo, which was at least two levels above my pay grade. It was the kind of restaurant that made me nervous. I felt as though everyone knew I was an impostor, and they were just waiting for me to make a fool of myself. Well, they didn't have long to wait. I was half way up the steps when my heel broke clean off. If that wasn't a sign from above, I didn't know what was. I couldn't possibly face Maxwell like that—I'd leave a message at the door—something had come up—an urgent case.

"Are you all right?" Maxwell said. "You're walking kind of funny."

No kidding Sherlock. "My heel snapped off."

"Have you hurt your ankle?"

"No, it's okay." Just my pride.

"Our table's over there. Here, take my arm."

"Thanks." He helped me to the table, and pulled out my seat.

"I wasn't sure you'd show." Maxwell took the seat opposite me. He had scrubbed up pretty well.

"We don't need to do this," I said. "We can call it quits now. No one need know."

"We're here now. We might as well at least enjoy the meal."

"Okay, but there's one thing I need to clear up first."

"Go on."

"The article in the Bugle. It wasn't what I'd agreed to."

He smiled, which unnerved me a little.

"It's true. I had the reporter's word that it wouldn't be a hatchet job, and that I'd have final approval."

"You trusted the word of a journalist?"

"Pretty stupid, eh?"

"Yeah. Pretty stupid." He laughed.

"I'm sorry if it embarrassed you."

He shrugged. "How about we agree to set aside our differences. Just for tonight at least?"

"Okay." After he'd let me off the hook for the Bugle article, it was the least I could do. "We can give it a go."

And we did. Much to my surprise the evening wasn't a complete disaster. The food was excellent, I didn't spill anything on my dress, and the two of us didn't come to blows. Under the circumstances, I considered that to be a result.

By the time it came to coffee, I was feeling much more relaxed. Maybe Kathy had been right — an unlikely scenario, I know — perhaps this would signal the start of a better working relationship between the two of us.

"So?" I teased "Is this the only way you can get a date?"

"Hey." He smiled. "Being the prize in the raffle wasn't my idea — I was pressured into it. Anyway, you can't talk. You must have been pretty desperate for a date, to buy a ticket."

"I didn't buy it. My sister, Kathy, did."

"I know, she told me. You do realise she rigged the outcome, don't you?"

"No!"

"Yes."

"How do you know?"

"I'm a detective, remember?"

"I'll kill her. Slowly and painfully. Rabid gerbils may be involved. So, why did you move to Washbridge anyway?"

"Circumstances."

Which was code for 'I don't want to discuss it', so I was happy to let it go.

"Did you hear about the Camberley kidnap?" he continued.

"The heiress? Yes."

It would have been practically impossible not to have heard about it, given the nationwide coverage that the case had received. Lorraine Camberley, daughter of the shipping magnate had been kidnapped, and was eventually found dead.

"I was lead detective on the case."

"The papers said the ransom was paid, but the kidnappers killed her anyway."

"The press didn't have the full story." Maxwell had reverted back to detective mode. I was beginning to regret having raised the subject. "Anyway," he continued after a few seconds. "After it was all over, I decided I needed a new start."

I sensed there was more to the Camberley story than he'd told me. Policemen saw death and tragedy all of the time—it went with the territory. Why had this case affected him so deeply? This probably wasn't the time to press him on the subject, so I tried to lighten the mood again. "So you decided to move to Washbridge? Centre of the universe."

He forced a smile. "What about you? Have you always lived here?"

"Pretty much."

"Any other family apart from your scheming sister?"

"My soon to be dead, scheming sister." I smiled. "I'm adopted. My adoptive parents are dead. Until recently it was just me, Kathy, and her family."

"Until recently?"

"Yeah. A few weeks ago, I made contact with my birth family for the first time. Now I have an aunt, cousins and a grandma."

"Do they live in Washbridge, too?"

"No, they live in—you won't have heard of it."

"Try me. I'm pretty hot on geography."

"Candlefield."

"You're right, I haven't heard of it. Where is it?"

Stupid, stupid, stupid! Why hadn't I given him the name of some other city?

"It's a long way from here. Up north somewhere. I'm not very good with directions."

Thankfully, he let it go at that.

"Can I give you a lift home?" Maxwell asked, as we left the table.

"It's okay, thanks. I have my car."

I carried my shoes, as we walked together through the lobby of the hotel. In my bare feet, he towered above me.

"I've enjoyed tonight," he said, as we reached the outer doors.

"You sound surprised." I laughed.

"Aren't *you*?"

I nodded.

"There is one thing I've been meaning to ask you," he said.

"What's that?"

"Who says you're a great kisser?"

I blushed so hard that I felt like my face might melt. During the 'Animal' case, I'd used the 'mind read' spell to try to get information out of Maxwell. To my surprise I'd found out that he was wondering what it would be like to kiss me. In a moment of insanity, I'd told him I was a great kisser.

"Err—I—err."

"Jill?

The voice came from behind me. I turned, and recognised the smile instantly.

"Drake?"

The two men stared at one another. My face was still burning hot.

"Jack, this is Drake Tyson. Drake, this is Jack Maxwell."

BOOKS BY ADELE ABBOTT

The Witch P.I. Series:
Witch Is When It All Began
Witch Is When Life Got Complicated
Witch Is When Everything Went Crazy
Witch Is When Things Fell Apart

AUTHOR'S WEB SITE
Http:www.AdeleAbbott.com

FACEBOOK
http://www.facebook.com/AdeleAbbottAuthor

MAILING LIST
(new release notifications only)
http:/AdeleAbbott.com/adele/new-releases/

BW July/16

JUN - - 2021 LN

NOV - - 2022 GR

Made in the USA
Middletown, DE
14 May 2016